Noora is a researcher of medical electronics at University College London and a graduate of New York University. She is interested in liberal arts, philosophy, and all sorts of fiction. One chapter of this novel was turned into a play that was presented at the university and received a lot of positive responses. Noora is originally from Dubai and enjoys sharing stories about people of the city.

To my loved ones, thank you for being present.

Noora Almarri

INFINITE ENDINGS

AUSTIN MACAULEY PUBLISHERS™
LONDON • CAMBRIDGE • NEW YORK • SHARJAH

Copyright © Noora Almarri 2024

The right of Noora Almarri to be identified as author of this work has been asserted by the author in accordance with sections 77 and 78 of the Copyright, Designs and Patents Act 1988.

All rights reserved. No part of this publication may be reproduced, stored in a retrieval system, or transmitted in any form or by any means, electronic, mechanical, photocopying, recording, or otherwise, without the prior permission of the publishers.

Any person who commits any unauthorised act in relation to this publication may be liable to criminal prosecution and civil claims for damages.

This is a work of fiction. Names, characters, businesses, places, events, locales, and incidents are either the products of the author's imagination or used in a fictitious manner. Any resemblance to actual persons, living or dead, or actual events is purely coincidental.

A CIP catalogue record for this title is available from the British Library.

ISBN 9781035809813 (Paperback)
ISBN 9781035809820 (ePub e-book)

www.austinmacauley.com

First Published 2024
Austin Macauley Publishers Ltd®
1 Canada Square
Canary Wharf
London
E14 5AA

Table of Contents

Who Tells the Story	9
The Wait	20
New York	24
Mornings	29
A Fool	33
Happy Eid	38
Scapegoat	46
Dianetics	53
Returning	58
Disturbing Sirens	61
False Memories	75
Deleted	77
Vibrations	82
One Hand, Five Dollars	86
False Palm	91
Grandpa	93
What Should Have?	97

Faded Feelings	99
Chances	104
Aristotle Lied	108
No Time to Grieve	115
Shadows	120
Coping Lies	124
Fake Identities	135
The Year of Death	137
Where Were You?	141
The Letters	146
2014	149
People Always Leave	154
I Wish	162
Goodbye	165

Who Tells the Story

AL

I tried to toy through my memories, I even polished the rusty ones. The last memory that rose is dull. It does not shine! My life all this time has been colourless. How can I toy memories when they are just a few?

The reasons for leaving home haven't fully crystallised in my mind. While I could conjure a list of possibilities, I prefer not to delve too deep. Perhaps it's due to her impending marriage—a union I once believed she'd call off. It all started with stumbling upon old letters, concealed by my brother. Curiously, these letters now accompany me to New York, though the purpose eludes me. Oddly enough, I'm not physically running; I'm confined to an aeroplane seat, suspended between places. Comparisons are inevitable—I'm more attractive, possessed of charm and finesse, yet she chose him, that boy! It's confounding; I'm a grown man!

The deep snores of the old woman sitting next to me break my concentration. I look around the plane; everyone seems to be sleeping in the dark even though it is daytime outside. I try opening my window to get some sunlight but it's slightly broken. It slips back down again and blocks my only source of light. I have no control over it. I have no control over anything anymore. I look back at my phone and delete the message because it doesn't sound like me. I do not speak like that to people, I am an educated man who knows what to say and what not to say. I brought a book on Plato with me, and he even reminds me of what I am escaping.

"As for the rest, we shall let those with sick bodies die. The citizens themselves will decide the fate of those whose minds have become warped and whose natures have become abnormal."

Plato's wisdom is stark. He advocated letting them pass on. A sensation familiar from clichés consumes me—I'm the tragic hero of an American movie, fleeing to New York City to outrun my past. What intriguing backstory should adorn my character? A wealthy scion escaping his affluent family in search of love, fame, or triumph? Yet, why the need to seek them out? Shouldn't they gravitate toward me? I once mocked such films, and now, I'm ensnared within their narrative.

I yearn for slumber to escort me until touchdown, but my mind's torrent resists even the lull of melatonin. Blame it on the vitamins I've ingested—agents of relentless wakefulness. Why do these supplements feel as taboo as illicit substances? This wasn't the script I envisioned; destiny intended me to thrive, to be a paragon of affluence and fame. How did I stray to this juncture? Reduced to embarrassment by a girl? My wit and charisma are undeniable, though some might label me self-assured. It's not arrogance, just an awareness of my worth. Yet, my essence transcends her—yet we were destined. I was fated to be someone, but now, I'm a mere nobody. The mantle of the next Elon Musk was mine to claim, not to settle for less. Why, in all creation, did she choose that mediocrity?

I strive to succumb to sleep, to trade this spiral for visions of the realistic "me" adored by all women. Yet, she infiltrates even my dreams. Don't misunderstand—I cherish her presence in my slumbers but lament the fading of those dreams, usurped by the mundane. I endeavour to recapture those elusive dreams, wishing for a glimpse of her once more. A pang of frustration—why do I lack her images? Women attach pictures to resumes, yet not on social media. What societal paradox excludes me? I yearn only to etch her features into memory. An innocent yearning fuels me—a yearning for connection, for her well-being, which I believe hinges on me. Now, back to our plotted narrative: I wed her; she avoids that loser, only to succumb to the clutches of depression. This, my fabricated truth, is it agreed upon?

Touching down at New York's John F. Kennedy Airport, the American flag gracefully drapes from the glass ceiling, a symbol of my newfound distance and uncharted territory. It's akin to Dubai's airport, and indeed, many others worldwide. Gathering my belongings, I spot three women conversing animatedly in Arabic, resembling my aunts. Their faces remain a blur, a conscious decision on my part.

Their voices echo within me, reciting, "We warned you, our traditions trump this modernity. You should've heeded our counsel and chosen a partner of our selection." My mother, in contrast, assured me of my liberty to pursue any woman I desire. A secret she's harboured: my father, too, maintains a second wife, under the pact that offspring wouldn't materialize from this union. Our distinction, our wealth, safeguarded within our lineage—purity resides with us. We're the inheritors of an unbroken legacy, unequivocally of this land. Yes, I recognize our country's youth, birthed less than five decades ago, yet my father predates its inception. I can vouch that my lineage, stretching through generations, is intrinsically rooted here.

MEDYA

Could someone please escort this delusional narcissist off the stage? Yes, I'm alive and well. His tangled thoughts are warping reality. Externally, he portrays someone else, but don't be deceived. Promise me you won't put your faith in him.

AL

She's a master manipulator. I, on the other hand, am candid with all of you. Trust that much. Consider astrology—our compatibility is apparent. She's an Aquarius, and I'm a Sagittarius. She chose to marry him, defying worldly plans, only to face the consequences decided by fate and the divine. It's a narrative woven perfectly, one that aligns with how stories should unfold. Have you ever seen a blockbuster movie rooted in astrology? Let's pioneer that. Nobody challenges destiny. I should be the storyteller, not her.

DIRECTOR

As you both insist, we must delve into both sides for deeper comprehension. But, Al, drop the superiority stance; it's racist.

AL

It's akin to "Animal Farm." Just like how some animals are more equal than others. We're merely "more equal," not necessarily better or superior. I never claimed that!

DIRECTOR

I believe readers are getting muddled regarding the play's essence. So, Al and Medya are contending to narrate this tale about…

MEDYA

He toyed with my emotions for months, talking about marriage, then abandoned me when his family deemed me unworthy. My father's incarceration isn't my doing. After that, he vanished for five years, only to resurface and mess with my head before I chose someone who offered security.

AL

I didn't vanish. I was waiting for the right moment to propose. Our time and specific moments gain significance from their finiteness, don't you think? They disapproved of my early marriage, my choice of someone from a lower class. I recall the day after I informed my mother of my intention to marry. She informed all my aunts, who convened at our home. I saw them talking, trying to sway my mother into arranging an Imam to recite Quran over me.

MEDYA

Lower class? You look down on me and anticipate acceptance? A bit of context: his mother is an unabashed racist. She disapproves of me due to my Russian heritage. She even humiliated the wife of Al's uncle by dressing her maids in the same attire as his uncle's foreign spouse. She thrives on mocking others' suffering—a true gold digger. I want no association with this man. She even tried to harm me. The issue lies in…

AL

That we love each other. Love is knowing everything about someone-the way she is going to style her hair, the dress she will wear, and knowing the exact stories she will tell in each situation. I know you more than anyone! Listen…

It is not my mother who is the issue… my aunts… her friends who I call my aunts. They think Medya used witchcraft on me to make me fall for her. I mean she got me to believe in astrology which is a kind of witchcraft, and she is poor so maybe she really wanted the money. But I didn't believe it because I am a good, charming man who loves her. I knew what was going on, it didn't require any witchcraft. The reality is the following: they just want me to marry one of their daughters. I didn't want to sit and talk to them that day, so I went to my room. I heard…

MEDYA
May I interject?

AL

She doesn't let anyone speak… Anyway, I heard a knock. It was Aunt Maha; she expressed her wish for a conversation. I mentioned sleep, but she saw through my ruse. She wanted to share just one thing, so I allowed her in.

She faced me, poised. "Al, I deeply care for you. I've witnessed you growing up alongside my son, Abdulla. You're like a son to me. I comprehend the turmoil you're grappling with, a transient phase. A phase wherein you're deceived by this 'love' concept. Understand, love is an illusion. Authenticity only emerges after marriage. Movies propagate an unreal narrative."

I remember the dialogue clearly; her assertions seemed utterly illogical. Out of respect, I merely nodded in agreement. She continued, "Marry logically, someone as affluent as your parents. Many suitors your grandfather rejected were only after our family's wealth. Al, you should heed me. Refrain from uniting with someone of modest means; marry within your social class. Remember our culture; adherence is essential. If a girl talks to a boy, she's questionable. If she converses with you, she'll likely betray you post-marriage."

Calmly, I gazed at her and countered, "Yet you divorced your husband for flirting with other women…"

Aunt Maha hesitated, then said, "It's a different circumstance. I didn't know him well prior to marriage; our first real meeting was at the wedding. Times have changed, now you get to know the woman and converse before tying the knot."

With certainty, I replied, "Aunt Maha, my plans are comprehensive. I'll marry her and study abroad in Germany together. Upon return, we'll secure respectable careers. I won't require assistance from my father."

She retorted, "In youth, we're oblivious to our genuine desires. I realize you're confident in your understanding."

"Can you please leave me be?" I implored. I knew my aspirations—constructing a future with someone I genuinely love. But what did she do instead? She divulged our family's secrets. She even ridicules my mother. Should we lend credence to her version, brimming with falsehoods? She deserves to fade, and I deserve to grieve and embark on anew. That seems fair.

DIRECTOR

If she were deceased, how would you continue the narrative?

AL

Well, that would be heart-wrenching. Devastating. Presently, I tend to follow my own advice, and right now I'd rather be anywhere else, confronting a world where people judge based on appearances, clothing dictating character. I usually offer myself sagacious counsel, yet at this moment, I question if fleeing was the right choice. Can we revisit the airport scene?

MEDYA

You're a master manipulator. Not to mention, quite tedious and dramatic. I disclosed everything in those letters! You simply didn't bother reading them, never seizing the chance to hear my side.

AL

Could you grant me a chance? To explain? Just sit back and watch the narrative unfold. I'll get to those letters. Remember, my brother concealed them. Their absence wasn't my doing. If you're still unconvinced that we're meant for each other, you can always leave midway. Just this once, extend me the chance to prove something.

MEDYA
One chance. One version.

DIRECTOR
Please proceed, Al.

AL

I find myself surrounded by those who aren't from Dubai, except for a tall, tanned guy, a spitting image of the man she married. A deep-seated urge to punch him takes hold. Familiar faces gradually vanish near the baggage claim. The instant I exit, a sense of liberation replaces those visages. A serene calm envelops me. Retrieving my phone from my backpack, I message my father. He'll inevitably share my news if inquired upon, or perhaps he'll claim I'm on a business trip.

Regardless, I remain indifferent. I text, 'Hey Dad, I'm relocating to New York for a few months. Need some time off work. No worries, I can handle myself.' My father calls as soon as I send the message, but I don't answer. I need solitude until I can harness my thoughts. He texts, inquiring if I require money—everything, to him, revolves around finances. My response is a resolute 'no.'

Playing her cherished song on my phone, the image of her at the piano flashes in my mind. Her smile, her exhilaration when discussing her adoration for music. She'd urge me to discern the tone, the lyrics, and most importantly, what it invoked within me. The internal echo and the song's external words. When I gifted her that jet-black piano on her birthday, she'd sit on the theatre stage, cascades of brown hair framing her, playing her favourite: Damien Rice's "9 Crimes."

Theatre is the place for illusion and yet the only place where people speak the truth. I knew she felt low when she played; her repertoire was all sombre tunes. No upbeat melodies—sad ones resonated, and made her feel more alive. She boldly pursued her dream of being a pianist straight out of high school.

I perused her writing on her modest blog—always melancholic, often unfinished. A trove of such works is uncompleted due to a lack of resolve. I did my best to prod her toward completion, leaving anonymous comments. Endings, it seemed, left her unsatisfied, akin to killing a fine piece with a lacklustre conclusion. That's why she preferred open endings. Presently, this scenario feels like one of her unfinished tales. I'm lost, directionless. Uncertain about the ending I seek for my own narrative. I grapple with the question of my purpose, akin to a 90-year-old burdened by the weight of an already traversed life. Yet, I'm only 27, with much ahead. And I must navigate it without her.

MEDYA

That wasn't even my favourite song. Every detail is being recast, a new painting with distinct hues. I'm done here. I'll leave you to your tale-spinning; people can decide if they believe your rendition.

DIRECTOR

I believe Medya should offer more detail about your initial encounter, what transpired between you, and how it concluded.

MEDYA

I encountered him in school. He reached out online as a girl, then promptly ignored me. Oh, and he circulated rumours prior to my wedding, insinuating I wasn't a virgin. Ridiculous, as I'd never even been close to a boy.

AL

I have no interest in discussing this nonsense. Let's return to the airport scene.

The Wait

AL

I drag my suitcase across the windy hallway to the taxi stop, then look frantically around. The line is never-ending, and everyone is busy on their phones. Will I ever reach my destination? Suddenly the song on my phone stops playing. It is dead. I need to recharge it. It shook me up when the music in my head stopped, bringing me back to earth. A nagging voice is coming from a little boy standing in front of me. Our eyes lock.

He gets bored immediately and continues his nagging rant. "Dad! Can we go today? Please, please, please!"

The father replies in a calm but exhausted voice, "Where?"

"Disneyland," says the boy with juvenile glee.

"The flight was long and Disneyland is not in New York."

The kid interrupted, "No! No! I want to go to Disneyland."

"We will go next week. I promise you."

The smell of gasoline polluting my nostrils brings me out of my daydream into reality.

I get into an iconic yellow taxi that has a shampoo ad hovering on top of it. Capitalism, I finally get it. I hate the medias; they are trying to control minds. It is very subtle, but it's the new form of fascism really. I'm glued to the seat; my back is thanking me after that 13-hour flight. The driver turns back at me and asks me with a straight face, "Where to, sir?"

I gaze at his old wrinkly face, grey hair, and big glasses. "11th street, 2nd avenue."

I try to smile, so he will think I'm nice. They like smiling here. Unlike back home, where they feel threatened or misled by a genuine attempt at sincerity. My face feels like dried mud. Smiling tires me. I am drained. Why am I so drained?

The taxi driver has kept his window open. I hate the smell of gasoline and this dying world, but I don't want to be rude, so I just stay quiet and lean on the window. It is daytime but the window is cold, it feels good against my skin. I miss the little things that felt good. I'm glad I shaved on the plane; my beard would've gotten in the way of this mesmerising feeling. I know I look as good as always. I look at the buildings from afar as we pass on the Brooklyn Bridge. The driver just keeps on looking at the rear-view mirror. He seems unsure whether to start a conversation with me or not. I guess the silence is itching him as he decides to talk.

Driver: "You from New York?"

Flattered, I respond, "First time."

Driver: "You don't say? Your moustache says otherwise!" He laughs hysterically.

"Heh," I replied.

"You don't look very excited about New York, if it was my first time, I'd have my head out the window like a wet dog on a summer's day."

I don't know how to respond so I sit straight, take my phone out of my pocket, then remember it's out of charge. I looked at the driver's rear mirror. He's no longer staring at me. Thank God he got the hint. It's 5:00 pm and the sun is still out.

The driver decides to fill the void in the taxi with 'America's top 10 hottest tracks on the radio'. I don't recall the song playing, but it makes me feel like I'm in a movie starring Ashton Kutcher and Cameron Diaz.

I can see the glassy skyscrapers standing high and mighty. There are bright red zigzag fire escapes covering the buildings. As the taxi passes through the neighbourhoods, I start seeing the people. I can see children playing on swings and their parents barely looking at them, as they are focusing more on their precious phones.

It takes me back to a time where we used to play on the swings for days. She was very ticklish; she would laugh like a maniac whenever I brought my hands close to her waist and her cheeks would turn flowery pink. She would hug me so tight that the only place where I could kiss her was her forehead. The memory brings a wry smile to my face. The taxi driver's voice interrupts my flashback.

"Sir... Sir... Sir... we're here... Sir."

"Sorry. Thank you."

I pay him, so I can get out.

DIRECTOR

Here it feels like you knew her when you were kids or teenagers. Above I was wondering when it was that you were reading her blog? Was that before you got together?

AL

It was after it ended. I was still there but not talking to her.

DIRECTOR
When did you play on the swings?

AL
When we were married. Remember this is the story I am telling. I married her then she died. Do you know how insane it would sound to still have feelings for a girl I barely dated? What would everyone think of me. I never hugged her, I never got close to her. How does a person have strong feelings that it could have worked when it is someone, they know so well yet they barely been with?

DIRECTOR
How long was the relationship?

AL
I will get to this part later. Can we get back to the New York scene?

New York

Oh, New York!
New York! New York!
I've never been here before
In my soul, my feelings are the same
But my entire life is about to change
Oh, New York! New York!
I want to be part of it all!
I want to be part of New York!
Colourful New York!
In the very heart of it!
I want to wake up in a city that doesn't sleep
And still, feel like the king
The king of the world
If I can make it here!
Then I can make it anywhere!
I will make it everywhere!
I will start new!

I think I have a potential to become a singer. I am very talented with words. Singing makes me feel more excited like I am in a movie. The building that I am moving to reminds me of an old movie. I am trying to remember the name of it, but such details do not really matter. What is important is the message behind the movie. Think about it. When someone tells you a great quote, does it matter who said it or the quality of the quote? I know a lot of people will disagree with me, and this argument can go on for days. All I can say is what I remember. The movie was about a girl that wanted to change or fix her life, so she took herself into a mental asylum instead of going to her dream college. I am signing myself into a mental asylum, but a fancier one. Without the crazy people that are usually there. Instead, I am alone. I am not crazy; I have full self-control over how I feel. I just cannot get her off my mind. I sometimes get distracted by simple details that I see around me, but she is always there, no matter what I do. How long is it going to feel this way?

My thoughts are interrupted by the porter's voice; "Hello, how can I help you?"

"I rented apartment 507 on the 5th floor, I am supposed to be moving in today," I reply.

"Sure, let me call the landlord," he replies with a smile.

He lets me into the lobby, so I sit in the waiting area. Meanwhile, he has taken my passport and asked me to fill some forms. I finish the necessary paperwork and, after waiting for 20 minutes, he gives me the keys. I carry my bag to the elevator in the lobby, pressing on the button. It turns out it is not working, so I have to take the stairs. I hate stairs, they complicate things. You can still get to where you want to go but with stairs it takes so much more effort and time.

I open the door of my apartment and see the kitchen counter next to the door. This place has hideous interior design. It is a studio apartment furnished with a kitchenette, a study desk, a blue couch, a single bed next to the window, and a washroom. It is the kind of apartment usually rented by college students, as they are cheap and small. I throw my bag on the couch and jump straight onto the bed with my shoes on.

The roof smells of mould. I already hate it here. I already have to call someone to get it checked but I really hope it is not mould. I don't think I even know what mould looks like. If my mother was here, she probably wouldn't stay in this apartment another minute. She even refused to move to our new house until she had been to Italy to pick the furniture. She likes everything to be fancy, especially since my dad can afford anything she could possibly ask for.

I don't recall being raised by her; I remember thinking that our nanny was my mother. Even when I was first in a relationship, I only told the nanny about her. My mother was a nice lady, but she was always somewhere else. I know that my father loved my mother a lot, so much that he didn't mind her being absent. He gave her everything she ever asked for. All the money that she ever wanted. It trapped her in her materialistic world. She was afraid of losing my dad's money more than she was of losing my dad. My father loved us all a lot. We travelled every year to fantastic places like the Maldives and Seychelles, and we spent summers in Paris. We didn't stay in any old hotel in Paris; it was always the most luxurious one because my mother wouldn't travel with us if we booked anywhere else. You would often see ministers and celebrities in the hotel's lounge. He was always there for us. I am more like him than my mother. My mother only gets involved in my life when one of the family had done something stupid. She was doing her job of protecting our legacy.

My thoughts are interrupted by the New York noise. I wonder how I will be able to go to work in such weather. Luckily, I won't be needing to do that until next week. I look through the window of my apartment, and see a homeless guy sitting in front of the building across the road. He is burying himself under a pile of blankets. It is the beginning of winter, so it will probably get colder.

I realise I am completely alone here. I love freedom, I love being carefree, and worry-free, I love being free! I love New York! I can finally be on my own. Alone, and away from all those restrictions, especially my mother's ones.

There are so many windows in the building in front of me. It seems like a workplace as I can see offices, but no one is there. The light is still on and there is only one coat on the hanger. Someone might still be there, but I don't see any movement. I need to stop looking, or they might report me as a weird stalker. I tend to analyse unnecessary details way more than I should. I try to link things that do not correlate, to reach an epiphany 'aha' moment. But I usually end up with nothing.

My schedule would be boring for the next few months. I would be busy working as a regional manager at Start NYC. I am looking forward to being the boss there. But I thought by this age, I would have started my million-dollar company. Why do all these losers get the things I deserve? I had high standards. High goals, high hopes for myself. Right now, I am feeling like Icarus. Dreaming too big, trying to escape the routine by building my wings. Trying to fly too near to the sun on wings that are made of feather and wax. Like Icarus, I couldn't escape the fall. The feathers came loose, and I plunged to my death. I escaped my prison just to be in another.

My thoughts are interrupted by the sound of my stomach rumbling. I have a skinny figure not because I eat healthy, but because I tend to forget to eat. I need to get out and grab some food before the supermarket closes. I am happy here. I feel better alone than when I am surrounded by people. If she is not with me, then I would rather be alone than with anyone else. The days here will distract me until one day I eventually won't think about her. Next to my coat I have put the only thing that is left from her: a box of letters. I feel the need to get away from it.

I grab my coat and walk to the elevator. But it is still broken. I'm clearly no longer living the life of luxury anymore.

Mornings

It is the morning!
It is the morning!
It has been several weeks, a month, or maybe a year!
The earth still revolving while my days are slowing.
Things are no longer feeling the same!
Days are dawning, I need to stop yawning!
I need to get up before I am late!
I see no birds!
The sky is very blue!
I see no birds!
The sky is very blue!
Early birds why are you always so late?
I cannot be late!
I have got to be there so soon!
I have been late for a meeting or two!
But it's okay I won't be late; I won't be late!

It is a normal day in New York City. I am late for work again. It is about time for me to get myself an alarm clock, maybe the classical 1920s' ones that come with a huge pendulum. I saw one of them in *The Great Gatsby*. I always thought of myself as Gatsby, trying to grasp the green light from the other side, where Rose lives. I mean, I am charming after all. Unlike Gatsby, I go after what I want. Also, Gatsby made his own money. I was born with it, or just around it. Maybe I am more like the other guy in that film, the guy who was Gatsby's neighbour. I forgot his name. Well, the only thing I do know is I have to work all day just like Gatsby's neighbour.

When I am finally done with work, I take a walk around Central Park. During the day, it is full of people singing and playing saxophone; at night the only thing you see there is people injecting themselves with needles to fill that emptiness within them. I hate needles, so instead, I just fill my empty chest with some fresh air. It goes into my lungs, and then just leaves.

As usual, I am thinking about my late wife, imagining her with a different mood every day. One day, I have made her sad. The next day, she is laughing with me. It is a rollercoaster of emotions. Sometimes I even forget that she is dead, and I try to text her. It is funny because, since no one paid her bill, her number has been taken by someone else. Now a random taxi driver is getting the 'I miss you' texts. Even at her workplace, she was replaced by another journalist as soon as she died. It's as though everything she ever wrote was just meaningless. The unfinished articles on her computer just got deleted in five minutes by the IT guy. Her nameplate on her desk just got tossed in the trash and replaced with another temporary name. We're mere cogs in a machine; if we falter, we're discarded and replaced with a shiny new component. The fortunate ones find themselves repurposed in a different machine, while the less fortunate remain discarded.

This is a random thought but sometimes, I just wish she had left me instead. Wouldn't that be easier? Wait. Wait. I take that back. She cannot leave me. I do not want to see her with another man. Her being with that other man and forgetting all about what we had! That cannot be right! She cannot forget all about me; I am her first love after all!

I need to stop this thought. I do not want to start shouting in the park, like a maniac. I won't shout. I won't. No one knows this, but I have a bad temper. The worst. But I hold it in so well, and that what makes me so charming to most people.

No one knows my fears or thoughts. That's why I refuse to go to therapy. Why would I want someone else to know how I feel and give me a list of flaws that they think they see in me. You are this, and you have that. In your childhood, you experienced x and y, and that's why you behave like the following. No, I have control over how I want to behave. There is no x and y. But deep down, I know that there might be an explosion of emotions. I need to find a way to be as solid as a rock, with no emotions as that would make my life a lot simpler.

The weight of these emotions grows heavier by the day. Ignoring them doesn't work anymore. So, I decided to shift to plan B, which is forgetting. Acting like it all never happened. My late wife who? I mean, I am still young and charming after all. Maybe I should chase beautiful young women all over again, and not let any emotions be involved because love is just like acid these days. Every drop burns and scars you. Wouldn't life be a lot easier without that acid being thrown all over the place? It is about time that I thought of her as something that I once had and that was taken away. Or maybe, just maybe I should make up a news story about myself and train myself believe it. And why just one story? I can wake up every day and tell a stranger a different extraordinary story that I just made up about myself. Like I was an astronaut, I was in the army, I can even say that I am a prince in my country. A different mask with a different character. Life could just be like a play in the theatre. You don't see actors expressing their true selves. It is all just acting, and I think it's about time that I join the play.

A Fool

There is a common misconception about people who don't blab about their emotions. They think that we are heartless. She thought I was heartless. I wasn't. I just hate talking over and over about how I feel about every single situation. In my head, my thoughts are saying everything she would want to hear. Every beautiful expression of love and support she has always wanted. In the end, she wouldn't believe me unless I somehow proved it so why waste time saying it. Am I wrong? She never gave me the chance to express how I was feeling. She would just have these outbursts, saying things I'd heard so many times I know them off by heart: "You will never care or be nice to me. You are so heartless! What did I ever do to you for you to treat me this way? Answer me. Don't just ignore me and walk away."

Every time we argued about anything, she would immediately explode and start breaking things. She even broke the beautiful china that my mother gave us as a wedding gift. Does she even know how much these things cost?

I never reply to her when she starts shouting. Instead, I just grab my jacket and leave. I never knew that a woman could become this crazy. I was doing the right thing because I truly cared about her. I did not want to say something heartless that she could use against me in the next argument.

But I was worried that I was not making her happy enough. I really didn't want to hurt this woman.

Even after everything that happened, I would go back after a while. Her mood would have switched, as though she was a completely different person. It was not my fault that she would switch moods so fast. She would come to me crying, telling me that she was sorry and asking me to never leave her. She was afraid of me walking away, but I wasn't going anywhere. I always tended to come back, and she knew that. I never said I would come back, but I never knew how to prove to her that I would.

I wish I could hold her. I wish I could lie down next to her and tell her that she will be okay. Everything will be okay. I am here. We are different, but I am here.

Mat, who works with me, passes by and notices that I am just staring at the computer like an idiot. I am there but at the same time I am somewhere else.

"Al... are you alright?" he asks.

"I am fine, just didn't have enough sleep last night. I have been exposed to American Netflix. Great shows, man," I say like a noob.

"Yeah cool! Cool! Just don't get too distracted with it," he says, in a kind voice.

He walks away but then comes right back. "Al... I almost forgot... our boss wants to meet with you. Like right now."

"Okay, thanks for letting me know." I nod, and stand up to go to his office.

I haven't really seen our boss since I started working here, because he was away for a while. Now that he is finally back, I need to make a good impression. I need to put on a new mask. As I walk, there is another little song that I was humming in my head…

> Over and over
> I will try to prove myself to you
> Over and over
> What more can I do?
> Over and Over
> I will be a fool for you!
> Because I will have no personality!
> A workaholic with no personality!
> A boring man with no personality!
> Just an extra with no personality!
> I will do whatever you say!
> Because I have no personality when it comes to you!
> So over and over
> Oh, I will be a fool
> A fool for you!
> I will do whatever you say
> What more can I do?
> I will be such a perfect fit
> With no personality!
> The perfect fit for a desk job!
> With no personality!
> Over and over!
> I will be a fool for you!
> What more can I do?

I notice him waiting outside his office door. As soon as I approach him, he gestures to me in a friendly way and asks me to take a seat.

"Welcome to the firm!"

"Thank you, boss," I smile back.

"I hope it was a smooth move to New York. So far, how do you like working here?"

"It is great. I am enjoying my time here, and I am starting to like New York."

"Good. Good."

"I forgot to say… Thanks… Thank you for offering me this job."

"You're welcome," he replies with a smile. Then he tries to continue the chat. "So, I see that you are from Dubai. I visited Dubai a couple of years back. That city amazes me as it keeps on changing with all the tall buildings."

"Yes, it does," I reply with a forced smile.

"I am originally from Yemen, but my family moved to the United States before I was born. You know my father was a taxi driver in Dubai; he said that foreigners can't be who they want to be in a land owned by the locals."

"Oh, that's interesting," I say.

"Aal… El… Al… Am I pronouncing your name, right?"

"Yes, you are. It is Al."

"It just doesn't sound Arabic to me. It is Ali, right?"

"Al is actually not my name, but it is the first two letters of my family name. When I was in school my teacher had difficulty pronouncing my family name and didn't call me by my first name since it is a common name in the Middle East. So instead, she called me Al. Then my friends started calling me Al as a joke, and then it just stuck with me."

"Most Arabs have an Al before their family name, how do people back home differentiate you from everyone else?"

I guess that, as Al I can be anyone back home, or just nobody here in the United States. That is the reply in my head, but I do not say it out loud. Instead, I try to come up with something that is less depressing.

"Well, most people would stick to their name," I reply.

"That's true, Al. Well, I am glad to have someone like you in my company. If you are facing any difficulty or anyone is giving you a hard time just let me know, my Arab friend."

"That is kind of you. Thank you." I stand up and walk back to my desk.

Happy Eid

Today is the first day of Eid. For the first time in years, I haven't had a text message from her. Back then, even if we were not in contact, she would still send me Eid greetings. That is how it was supposed to be. Every year, I would unblock her before Eid for a couple of days just to receive an Eid message from her. Instead of replying, I would block her again because I don't want her to feel like she is in charge. Why would I do that? Well, because her messages were overwhelming... I mean, what was I supposed to say? It was clear she was obsessed with me, but I was not sure what I wanted yet. I cared too, but back then I wasn't prepared to commit to her. I didn't know what I wanted to do in my career, so how could I think about having a wife? I couldn't just drag her with me after everything that had happened between us.

She always assumed that I was ignoring her, but I wasn't. I read her messages over and over again even while she was blocked. I was just going through a lot of stuff in my life. But she never understood me. She said it herself; I am unpredictable, which is a good thing as I am full of surprises. I thought it was clear that it was just not the right time, can't she just wait for me?

I wish I had said something to her, but I was afraid of losing her. It seemed better to keep her waiting for me, than to let her walk away with someone else. Well, frankly I knew she would be waiting for me. She couldn't walk away from me, because we were meant to be together, after all.

I know she can't be with any other man. She will never be able to love anyone else. She will always come back.

Lately, I have been reading about the idea of soulmates. She always thought that we are soulmates, but I think she was wrong. We were actually twin flames. My soul and hers are supposed to be one. Twin flames are two different people who, when they meet for the first time, experience everything they do together intensely. They feel like they have known each other for a very long time. It's like they have met before, in every past life. Every moment feels intense, every feeling is intense, and all their arguments are intense. Letting go of each other is intense. And now that she is no longer here, in spirit she is supposed to be close to me, if the whole idea of the twin flame is true.

On the other hand, maybe we weren't twin flames, because the whole thing was more complicated. Your twin flame is a person who makes you grow in some kind of way. We dealt with situations differently. She had zero control of her feelings, and I thought everything through before saying anything.

The more I think about it, the whole idea of reincarnation, soulmates, and twin flames just seems crazy to me. My body feels like the only real body I have ever had. This mind feels like the only mind I have ever had. My wife was obsessed with reincarnation, astrology, and soulmates. Sometimes I felt like I had married a hippie. She used to buy crystals that were crazy expensive to protect us from negative energies and the evil eye. Some of the crystals she bought looked nice as decorations, but I refuse to believe in these kinds of bullshit. These crystals didn't protect her from death. They were just a waste of money.

I find myself at home, perched by the window of my apartment, quietly observing the hustle in the office that stares back at me. My focus drifts to the coats still suspended there, an unintended tally of monotony. Boredom has woven its threads through my days. Recent weekends have witnessed me sprawled on my bed, the day slipping by to the tune of a shuffled playlist on YouTube. The music transcends language, not confined to English alone but embracing French melodies as well. Sometimes, I muse about reciting French lyrics, perhaps masquerading as someone with a French identity. I possess a lanky build, my skin carrying a touch of pallor. At times, I contemplate whether I could pass off as a Frenchman, given my height and complexion.

The thought makes me smile at my absurdity. I am becoming a mad man.

The letters persistently occupy my thoughts. A relentless refrain echoes in my mind: "Dispose of the letters!" When these ruminations mount, I recognize it's time to step away from my apartment.

Around 6:00 pm, a habitual ritual unfolds—an aimless stroll through the neighborhood. At times, I'm lost in the pulse of music emanating from my phone, while on other occasions, I find myself eavesdropping on the conversations of strangers who walk alongside me.

New Yorkers say "like," almost ten times in a sentence. It is hilarious how shitty their English can be.

While walking, I come across *The Bean* and think about grabbing a cup of coffee. My usual order is a flat white with almond milk. The café looks crowded from the outside. I see a child eating a chocolate cupcake with the chocolate frosting all over his face. His mother tries to clean his cheeks with a tissue but some of the tissue sticks to his face. I love kids. I really wish I had one; at least it would distract me.

Oh, no. I don't want a kid; I don't have the energy to raise him or her. I just like other people's kids. They would be easier to cope with if they came with a switch, an 'on and off' button on the back. Then, as soon they start crying you could switch them off, and when you need someone to cheer you up, you could switch them back on. It would be great if they also came with strings to control them, so that they wouldn't run away like idiots. A dog would be easier to cope with but, it would still shit everywhere.

I decide to go in. As I wait for my usual coffee, I hear a woman sitting behind me saying, "Being sad makes you creative."

"No, no. Sadness makes you lazy and unable to do anything," a man replies. He is wearing a white sleeveless shirt and I can only see his back.

I look back at them and hear myself saying, "Sadness can be controlled if you suppress those urges."

The man with the white sleeveless shirt turns around, so I can see his old grumpy face and grey beard. I notice that his eyes are wide open and so is his big smile. My eyes shift from his face to his wrinkly arms. I wonder why he isn't wearing a long-sleeved shirt? I really hate staring at his wrinkly arms.

He looks at me and says, "What do you mean suppress? How do you do that? Have a seat… you need to tell me how you do that!"

Why did I say something? Do I really want to talk to these strangers? Do I even have the energy for it? I notice the old man's eyebrows are raised. He looks worried that I will reject the invitation to give him a huge explanation. His face is begging me to tell him what the key to happiness is. So, I just walk over with a fake smile. God, I hate social interactions. There are like five people sitting. What will sitting with a bunch of strangers help me with? A brown woman with dark brown hair and colourful long earrings grabs a chair and makes space for me to sit down. She is wearing thick eyeliner and red lipstick. She seems to be in her thirties. She is kind of attractive. Ugh, I miss women.

"My name is Lulu and I work as a librarian in the Cottage Cheese library in North London. I am only here for a couple of weeks for a vacation. A fun fact about me is that I really enjoy writing children's books." She looks at me with a smile.

Another man interrupts and says, "Hold on… Hold on… I think he is confused by us introducing ourselves like this. Are you familiar with the website meetup.com?"

"Me? Well, not really… what exactly is it?" I actually have no idea what he was talking about.

Another guy who looks Japanese says; "Well, it is a website that lets you meet people who have a similar interest as you. You create an account, and then you can see the list of events happening close to you. You can sign up for an event near you."

"So, what is this meeting about?"

"Well, this is a meeting for people who have been diagnosed with bipolar, depression, or even both disorders. We meet in a different place every couple of weeks."

Jesus. What did I get myself into? Another person in the group continues the conversation, but I am not really listening to most of them because I don't really care what they do or what their names are. I am probably never going to see any of them again.

Lulu looks at me and asks me to introduce myself to the group.

I look at her and say:

"My name is Max, and I work at Target."

I don't know why I lie about my name, but does it really matter who I am today. It is just another mask that I can wear for today. Today I am Max, tomorrow I will be Zack, Felix, or even Shady. Who cares what my name is? I can be whoever. In fact, names have no significance at all, they are just temporary labels that you do not choose. Then, as soon as you are no longer present, these labels are given to someone else. They are not even special to you; there might be ten other people who have the same label. They have the same name and last name. Nothing so special about you. The only thing that separates you from other people is your ID number. Not your name, because it is not special at all.

"What do you enjoy doing, Max?" asks Lulu.

"Well, I like jogging." I lie.

"That's nice. I used to jog around Hyde Park to release the built-up stress that was caused by my family. But It didn't really work with me because, when I am done jogging, and I get home. I feel so tired, and being tired makes my depression worse," says Lulu.

"I feel the same way when I am depressed, especially since my girlfriend left me," says the guy who looks Japanese.

"Is this like an AA meeting?" I ask.

"Well, kind of but we are more open because we meet in different places every time. These meetings have given me an insight on the different behaviours people with depression display," says Lulu. "I am a Scientologist, and I follow the teachings of L Ron Hubbard. I have been doing this new kind of therapy that called Dianetics," says one of the guys.

"What is Dianetics?" I ask.

"Well, it is like you meet with an auditor who helps you unfold gathered traumas. You need to get rid of these traumas in the unconscious mind that might be controlling your day-to-day actions," he says.

"That sounds interesting. But if it works, why are you here?" I ask savagely. I don't mean to be rude, but it just came out without me thinking.

"Well, humans are like trees; they need constant care and nurturing to grow. You cannot water the tree once and expect it to continuously grow," says Lulu.

"Happiness is the highest level of Scientology's teachings. It is when you reach the mental state of clear. That's when you are no longer controlled by any outside factors," says the guy.

The guy who looks Japanese responds: "Dianetics doesn't work for me because I do not open up easily. It takes time for people to open up. It took me a year, and, when I did, the panic attacks that I used to get every night slowly decreased. I think when you let emotions build up, they become heavy… really… really heavy."

I nod.

The meeting doesn't last much longer. I walk out thanking the group for letting me join them. Before I leave, I walk Lulu all the way back to her subway stop. While I am talking to her, I swear she starts to look like my wife. Even her voice started to sound like her. She is captivating, and I am so lonely. I try to get her number, but she says she is leaving for the United Kingdom. She must be married; otherwise she wouldn't be able to resist my charm. She leaves, and I walk the other way to a bus stop.

I am still trapped at the moment when Lulu left. The sound of the cars starts to bother me. I take out my phone and plug my headphones in to drown my thoughts. I feel really alive when I want something or someone for more than just basic survival needs. I mean, whether it is intimacy with another person or just sitting in a café and chatting about philosophy and life. It's kind of beautiful to still have these ever-renewing desires. Not knowing what it could have been with an absolute stranger bothers me so bad. I mean, the point of life is looking, search, to stay hungry for meaning, right?

Scapegoat

I am tired of talking to myself and chasing strangers hoping that they are her. They might feel like her at the beginning, but I am starting to realise that they are not. I have to go talk to someone. My friend, Aisha, recommended a counsellor who she used to go to when she was taking a study abroad semester in New York. Her name is Dr Veronika Walker. Her office is in East Village, Manhattan. I don't need to go to her, but I am just bored, and I want to have some excitement. I hope she is as good as the Yelp reviews suggest, which is that she is one of the best therapists in the Big Apple…

I walk into her office…

Dr Veronika: Hello, Al, thank you for coming.

Al: Thank you for having me.

Dr Veronika: Have a seat.

Al: Are you playing some music in the background?

Dr Veronika: This is my meditation and healing playlist; it helps people recall memories more vividly and connect to their inner self in the sessions. Anyway, you can have a seat on the couch. If you feel more comfortable lying down, please do. This a free space.

Al: I think I might just sit.

Dr Veronika: Sure. What do you want to talk about?

Al: All my life, I have been trying to escape my problems and my fears, but I have reached the end. The part when all my fears have come to life or to be more specific, all my dreams have died. My wife is dead, and I am more lost than ever. Also, there are these letters haunting me.

Dr Veronika: What letters?

Al: I see these letters waiting for me to open them. They are the only things I have that is left from her and what makes it scarier is that I do not know if all of them are addressed to me. I don't know if I have the right to read them. Also, I do not know if these letters are going to make me crazy.

Dr Veronika: It is good that you are processing all the possibilities. Where did you find these letters?

Al: After she died, her mother was so devastated that she couldn't handle staying in the same house, so she decided to move. She asked for my help emptying her daughter's room because she was afraid she would find it too emotional. We brought a couple of boxes and placed her daughter's clothes in it for charity. She had a small bookshelf. It had a bunch of files that were colour-coordinated based on the subject: yellow for chemistry, blue for biology, red for mathematics, and much more. I read the title of each file until I found the last file, the purple one, that was hidden at the bottom of the pile.

Dr Veronika: What did you do with the files?

Al: I opened each of them and tossed the papers in the recycling bin, except for the writing file. I knew that the writing file had a few of the fiction pieces that she wrote while she was in high school, but never finished...

Dr Veronika: Are you remembering something?

Al: Well, at first, I thought it contained her pieces of writing... you know the ones that she forced me to read. But when I opened the folder... there weren't any.

Dr Veronika: Was it empty?

Al: No.

Dr Veronika: What was in the folder?

Al *sigh*: There were just some envelopes in the file. I held one of them and it didn't feel empty. That's why I opened it right away, and it had a letter addressed to me in it. I panicked and put the letter back in the envelope. Then I tossed all the envelopes in a plastic bag. Her mother walked in on me and asked me what I had in my hands, but I panicked. I didn't know what to say. Should I have told her that I was freaking out over finding those letters? And God knows when where they written, or what was in them...

Dr Veronika: What did you do next?

Al: I didn't think about why I wanted the letters. I didn't know if it was a good idea to take them, but I just did because I panicked.

Dr Veronika: What will you do with them?

Al: I just do not believe in coincidence, you know; I think life is just some kind of an unending story, with endless twists. It was like I was meant to be in that room. I have to admit that I am scared of what she would have to say in them, and why she didn't send me the letters.

Dr Veronika: Was there a time when your wife didn't tell you something?

Al: She tends to hide her feelings a lot. Anyway, there are 11 letters, which I numbered when I opened the envelopes. They were numbered from zero to ten. I brought them home and left them in a box under my bed.

Dr Veronika: So, you brought them with you to New York?

Al: Well, yes. That's the whole point... the plan is to throw them off the Brooklyn Bridge at the end of the trip and erase her from my memory.

Dr Veronika: You do realise that feelings should be processed not suppressed. Explored not dismissed. You are not a robot, Al.

Al: What are you trying to say? Will I forever be tortured by that pain?

Dr Veronika: No. What I meant is that you have got to let it out. Feel the emotions until they no longer have power over you. If you just let them in, they would take control over you.

Al: What do you think I should do with the letters?

Dr Veronika: Maybe we can read them together?

Al: What if it makes the situation worse?

Dr Veronika: We can always analyse and process everything together.

Al: Thanks. Do you know what my biggest struggle is?

Dr Veronika: Tell me.

Al: It is when I lay in bed. I remember every detail from when we first knew each other to the end... each memory feels like a stone thrown on my chest. When this happens, it becomes hard to breathe. It is hard. You know... memories keep on playing in my head. It keeps on replaying every night like I am in a movie called; *This Is How Al Ruined His Life.*

Dr Veronika: I think you might be experiencing some panic attacks.

Al: I don't think that's what they are. It is just normal, you know.

Dr Veronika: Al, close your eyes.

Al: Okay.

Dr Veronika: What do you feel right now?

Al: I feel sudden anger. Like I want to punch someone or break something. But I do not want to kick the table.

Dr Veronika: Why won't you?

Al: Because it is not proper manners to do that.

Dr Veronika: Just let it out. You can kick the table if you choose to speak while kicking.

Al: I am not angry.

Dr Veronika: Your face says otherwise.

Al: I hate how judgmental people were and what they did to ruin my life.

Dr Veronika: When?

Al: Our school wasn't like the typical high schools in American movies. The funny thing is that it was called an American school. But it was gender-segregated into two buildings: the boys' section and the girls' section. The girls and boys are not allowed to talk to one another or else they would get in trouble or even get expelled for any kind of communication. It didn't make any sense because once we got out of school… you know; the real world is different.

Dr Veronika: Then why was the school segregated?

Al: You see. They thought we were young and stupid. They told the girls stories like: "Oh a girl once talked to a boy from the boys' section and he told his friends, so they kidnapped her, cut her into pieces, put her in a black trash bag and threw her in the desert."

Dr Veronika: And what do you think of such stories?

Al: Absolute bullshit. If that was true, then it is not the girl's fault. I don't get why they use fear to stop people from making mistakes, can't we just learn from our own mistakes?

You know what is funny about all of this? Some people are still racist and do not accept interracial marriages. Back home, people want to know if your great... great... great... grandparent was from the same family. Oh, if his great grandmother was not an Arab then he is not good enough for them! No one is ever good enough for anyone!

Dr Veronika: How does that make you feel?

Al: Angry. Really angry at how backward-thinking people can be.

Dr Veronika: Did any of this affect any of your decisions?

Al: To those kinds of people, I am perfect. I am from perfect breeding, rich, handsome, the right degree of white. That's what I am, a true Arab. As a man in Dubai, I should be proud of my family for keeping this legacy, and not destroying it through emotional decisions. And of course, you know who failed them. I did. I am always the failure of this family.

Dr Veronika: So, what was the school like?

Al *sigh*: Since most parents did not have the time to pick up their kids from two different doors, the school decided to use one exit that wasn't gender segregated but there were teachers all around to prevent anything from happening. We had so many parents snitching on girls who did not cover their hair or boys who wear bracelets. In that school, no one minded their own business. The counsellor in the boys' section would ask the boys to go home and not come back if their hair was too long.

Dr Veronika: Did you ever speak to your parents about changing schools to an international one?

Al: Most people in Dubai put their kids in this type of school because it is religiously strict, which is the way they like it. In fact, people there were judgmental hypocrites. They would say one thing and then do something else. They would make promises that they didn't keep. I guess with all these rules, I never thought that one day I would actually feel free.

Dr Veronika: Are you angry at the school?

Al: No. I am angry at the people there for not knowing any better.

Dr Veronika: Okay, time is up. I will see you again in two days. Al, I would suggest you take a long walk around the park tomorrow if you have any free time, okay? And write down how it makes you feel.

Al: Can't I just pay for one more hour?

Dr Veronika: I am sorry, Al; I have a patient after you. Alba, could you please book him another appointment for tomorrow or the day after.

Al: Thank you. Have a nice day.

Dianetics

I have been thinking about this new kind of therapy that the AA group were talking about, Dianetics. According to Google, it can help me erase unwanted memories that can interfere with my happiness and sanity. Some say it is like a cult. I have been thinking about trying it out. I found the address for a Scientology church in midtown Manhattan. I tend to enjoy trying new things, and while this sounds crazy, only an hour after finding the address, I find myself standing in front of the church.

The people there welcome me with enthusiasm. They ask me to sit and watch a short trailer about how some people can be subconsciously affected by past traumatic events, which can be recorded as memories in our subconscious mind, also called the 'reactive mind.' Later, our mind reacts to future events in an illogical way because past experiences trigger our response.

Then I pay in advance for a session with a Latina woman called Laticia; she is supposed to be my 'auditor' in this whole weird experience. She asks me to sit and then starts speaking. She tells me that she learned all of this in Spanish, so she is not very fluent in English, but her English seems fine.

Laticia: You are fully aware of everything that happens during the session. In the future, when I utter the word cancel, everything I have said to you while you are in the therapy session will be cancelled and will have no force on you. Any suggestion I may have made to you will be without force when I say the word cancelled. Do you understand?

Al: Yes.

Laticia: Close your eyes.

This is creepy, but I close my eyes. I have no choice.

Laticia: Thank you. Locate an incident that you feel extremely happy in. Go through the incident and say what is happening as you go along.

Al: When I first saw her walking outside to the school's main gate… it was the first time I ever saw her.

Laticia: Can you recall any more details. Who was she? What was she wearing?

Al: The school uniform; a blue long skirt, and a white shirt.

I pause for a while seeing everything vividly. It feels like I can see her right there.

Laticia: How does seeing her make you feel?

Al: Like everything suddenly stopped. I couldn't feel the heat of the sun. I couldn't hear the teacher shouting at the students who were running around. I couldn't see the flowers in the school's garden. I was too focused on her.

Laticia: Was she looking at you?

Al: Nope, she wasn't.

Laticia: Go over it again and tell me what is happening as you go along.

Al: I was wearing a grey t-shirt instead of the school shirt. I liked punk rock. It was the last months of eighth grade before the summer vacation. It was around 2:00 pm. I had just finished one of the midterms, I think it was mathematics.

I pause again.

Laticia: Continue.

Al: She was the most beautiful girl I have ever seen. I was afraid of falling for her. Ugh… why am I tearing up?

Laticia: What are you afraid of?

Al: When I first saw her, everything just suddenly paused for few seconds. I stopped walking and kept looking at her and then I was hit on the head by the school's administrator. He told me to not look at girls or else I would get in trouble. After that day when I first saw her, the only thing I would focus on in class was the clock above the chalkboard. I would look at it while I was waiting for time to pass. Time would pass so slowly, but as soon as I saw her the time just flew by.

Leticia: Experience the feeling you felt that day.

Al: I don't want to cry; I am a grown man.

Leticia: Go over the incident again and say what is happening as you go along. Do you recall any smell, any sound, any other detail?

Al: There is nothing else that I can recall.

Leticia: It is necessary that you go over it again. Just one more time.

Al: My elder brother, who was a year older, liked this girl who he thought was pretty; he spoke to us about her. He wanted to show us that girl, and when he did, it was her, the first time I see the girl. From the moment I saw her for the first time I felt that she was my type, very pretty. I felt I could get her if I wanted to; she was like this forbidden fruit that I needed to grab before my brother. She was mine, not his. I felt a different sort of connection to her. Yes, everything around me stopped for a few seconds. I felt a burst in my chest, like I had accomplished something amazing, but I needed to do something. I needed to get to her before anyone else.

Leticia: How do you feel about it now?

Al: I know her better than anybody else, I see everything, and I focused a lot on her body movement. I could feel when she was sad, I could feel when she was happy. Our souls are connected in some sort of way.

Leticia: How do you feel about it?

Al: Good. I got what I wanted.

Leticia: That's good. Now locate another incident where you felt extremely frustrated. Go through the incident and say what is happening as you go along.

Al: We stopped communicating and then, after some time. I saw her at our graduation. We were strangers again, but I was still in love with this woman. I didn't see her for a very long time, but I was stalking her social media. I even thought she had moved from our school. However, everything changed on graduation day when our eyes met again in the huge auditorium room. Suddenly, everything paused again for few seconds. It was like the first time I met her; I felt like the world was telling me she was the one because in that crowd everything else was blurred. She was the one I wanted to spend the rest of my life… and then she turned the other way. I knew she couldn't stare in my eyes for too long. I knew deep down that she felt the same way, I was so sure of it. I didn't want my thoughts to stop me from what I was about to do but they did. I couldn't move my feet; it was as if they were nailed to the ground. I didn't care about anyone in that room, because she was the only one I could see. However, every time I tried to take a step near her the weight of my legs just got heavier and heavier. When we tell people about our proposal, we always tell them that...

I found myself walking up to her and looking into her dark eyes, saying, "You are the one I want to spend the rest of my life with. You are the one I want to be with when all my dreams come true. I love you."

We would say that she had stared at me dumbfounded. We would say that she looked down at her feet for a moment before facing me again and wrapped her arms around me. The auditorium would be noisy but when she hugged me, everything just paused again, and everyone was staring at us... but we just didn't care. We'd say her mother was confused, and she asked about who I was. But... but that is not what happened that day.

Leticia: Then what happened?

Al: The memory is replaced with a blur. I didn't go to her; I couldn't do it. What would society, and all the people in that room think of me? What will my friends think? I didn't want to lose them. Yes, at that moment it might have felt that this might be the last time that I would ever see her again. But if it was meant to be, then it would work out by itself, right?

Leticia pauses for a second.

Al: I can't see her because my eyes are closed.

Leticia: Go over the incident again, try to add more details. Anything that you can recall.

Returning

I had one chance. I ran into her in public a couple of months after graduation. I couldn't do that again. I couldn't let her leave. I grabbed her hands.

"Let go of my hands, we are in public!" she yelled.

"Wait! We really need to speak... can we sit. I will get you coffee, I know you love coffee."

"I have waited for almost two years, Al, to hear something from you, an explanation, anything. I waited for the perfect parting line. For some kind of closure. An ending to what we once had. Yes, I have loved you... more than you can ever imagine. But it is about time that I start thinking with my head rather than my heart. Al... You never gave me an explanation. You just left and expected me to find some sort of clues. I can't read your brain, and you just kept on avoiding us having any sort of meaningful conversation. I have always tried to imagine what I would say if I ever saw you one more time... I've wondered, what will Al have to say for himself? I repeatedly thought about scenarios in different locations, in different years. What will Al have to say to me? What is the excuse this time?"

"Can we at least sit down?"

"Al, we have been together for months then you would cut me off without even saying why. Just like that in the middle of a conversation. Then months later, you would walk back into my life, and then cut me off again like I mean nothing! You know what is attractive? Stability and that is the only thing you could never give me. I asked myself for years what I do wrong for you to cut me off every time so brutally. The sad part is when you come back, I would let you back in because..."

"Because what?"

"Are you ashamed to let the whole world know that you broke my heart? Unlike you, Al, I do not care what anyone would think of me anymore because you destroyed that part of me. I am being myself, and you walked away from me when I needed you the most. Then you came back, then what? You walk away from me again and again. I can never let you be in my life again; I am done with getting betrayed. You never fully let me in. I am sorry, but I need to go..."

"You know that you love me, and you would always choose me. I was waiting for the right moment to ask you."

"To ask me if you broke my heart? You did and it was hard losing you and it is really hard seeing you again." She started crying.

She was like a chandelier, beautiful to have around, but very fragile and requiring special care to avoid breaking it. It was hard for me, but I knew it was the right time to propose. I didn't want to get married. I wasn't ready, but I had no choice. I knew she loved me and she wouldn't say no. I needed to do it now; she could not reject me. She could not do this to me.

Someday you will meet someone and suddenly everything will align perfectly. You won't hesitate or even question yourself about it. You will love unconditionally, without the fear of failure. Everything will just make sense. Love can be the most beautiful thing or the most painful thing. Like sunlight, sunset, we appear and disappear. We are important to some, but at the end we are just passing through to all.

I am back home after the dianetics session. Right now, the silence is stifling. I can't sit still. My apartment seems bigger or wider than it has been over the past few months. Is this how it feels to be alone? They leave us, turning our life into a void, and the world becomes a void, a meaningless boring wasteland.

There is this moment that keeps on playing in my head. It makes no sense. It is hard to write about it, as I feel like memories are heavier on some days than others. It is so hard to recall a moment, even though it is just a simple moment when I was with her. Sometimes I feel like I want to forget her, and other times I feel like I want her around for just a few more minutes. I want to have more memories of being with her, there is so much I wish had happened.

I lied about marrying her. It just makes me feel better to say that I did. Isn't it easier to move on that way? It won't make sense to anyone that I am grieving this much for someone who is alive. Someone I never was able to really be with. Pain sounds more painful when you really cannot do anything about it. I can't do anything about it because she married someone else. She chose someone else. How can she let go of all the love she once carried for me? She claimed to be deeply in love, yet she chose to marry that loser. He isn't better than me in any way, but she still chose him. She couldn't just wait. She couldn't.

She should leave him anyway. I am sure he will never be able to make her heart vibrate the same way I made it vibrate.

Disturbing Sirens

The fire alarm is piercing my ears. I hate unexpected loud noises. I wasn't doing anything interesting, so it doesn't really matter at this point. I am pretty sure it is just fake news, and everything is just fine. Should I even bother leaving my apartment at this point? Maybe I should give it, like, five minutes, and then maybe do something. If it was a real fire... but that is very unlikely because people tend to exaggerate everything. But if it was a real fire, like in the movies, then the whole building would be covered in flames. And if I left, I would be running to find the nearest emergency exit, then I would realise that I forgot to take the letters with me. Would I be the person who goes back into the flames to get the letters, or would I let them burn and blame it on the unexpected cinematic coincidence. Would it be a sign from the universe that I am not supposed to read them?

Five minutes have already passed. I grab my phone from the charger to check the time. I think I should leave this apartment before the fake fire burns it down. I look up at the mould on the ceiling just to avoid looking at the letters. They are just there on the table waiting for me to take them with me.

I look down from the window to spot the ambulance that is also piercing my ears with its loud siren as the cars give it a way forward. I pick up the blue box filled with her letters from my desk and leave the apartment. As I hold the box, my hands feel numb and all sounds go mute. I feel the urge to open the box overcoming my fears. I take a deep breath and close the door of my apartment.

As soon as I get out of the building, I notice everyone outside shouting at an old guy. I can't really work out what he did, but I think he somehow set off the fire alarm. Maybe he caused the fire if there was one. I still do not know. I do not see anything burning but there are firefighters going into the building.

To avoid the noise, I decide to walk away to a café two blocks from my place. It is a bubble tea cafe, that looks dull. That is the thing about New York, most places are either really fancy and aesthetic or really dull and boring. Dull cafés are usually empty, as they are meant to be for the rats of the city. You peek into these dull restaurants, and the people look like rats holding the menus that have stains of ketchup all over them. Every place is pre-labelled, so you can judge a place before even going into it. I wish humans were labelled too. Grade A, B, C, D, E, and F. But then everyone would want A, and no one would dare to try F. Even the people who handed out those labels, wouldn't change the label of F, because once you are labelled something, then even if the label changes, the letters would stay in people's head. The best thing is for restaurants rated F is to be left for the rats, and restaurants A, B, and C can be left for the people.

I go in and order myself a bubble tea with peach. I am not a big fan of bubble tea. I feel like I am eating plastic, and the aftertaste is unpleasant. But I still order it. I sit and look at the box of letters. The letters were not in order, so I numbered them from 0 to 10. I pick the letter 0. I notice that there is something written with very small handwriting in scarlet red. So, I start to read the short note on the envelope.

This is my last letter, but I think it should have come before all the other letters. I do not want any response from you. If you ever plan to read this, read this one first, and listen to Trespassers William's 'Lie in the Sound' while reading it. Actually, do not listen to this one… listen to Hoobastank's 'The Reason'… this feels like our song.

I cannot listen to music and read at the same time. It is just so hard to concentrate on the words of the song while reading. I will just listen to the song first, and then read the letter when I feel ready. Will it harm me if I just listen to the song today? It could not be considered reading. I am just not ready to read anything from her. I know that these letters are most likely love letters, or maybe depressing, 'blaming it all on me' kinds of letters. I cannot really tell what they will be. I hate how I sometimes overthink everything that I am about to do. Sometimes I wonder why I can't just do something without feeling the need to imagine every possible scenario. What can possibly go wrong? She is already gone. I grab my phone, search for the song on YouTube and hit on the play button. My left leg starts to shake, as it usually does when I am about to make a major decision. I sometimes wonder if it is God trying to stop me from making a stupid decision. It is just a song; it could be playing in the restaurant without me even knowing that it has some sort of significance. That makes me realise I can just ask the guy working here to play the song over the speakers since I am the only customer here.

He starts playing the song and tells me that the song is actually from the soundtrack of a TV show called *One Tree Hill*, that he used to watch while he was in high school. It kind of made sense; she probably got inspired by the show, and decided to write this letter. It is not my kind of music. The tone isn't depressing as I expected; instead, it is somehow different. It is hard to explain how it makes me feel. I guess it is a bit hopeful with some weird sense of comfort… I never heard her play this song when we were living together. She wanted me to watch *One Tree Hill* with her. I managed to watch one episode, but the quality wasn't HD, it was just too annoying to watch something that was unclear especially with a million advertising pop-ups on the screen. I promised her that I would watch it once I ordered the CDs, but she hates waiting so she just spoiled the entire show for me. It is pointless to order the CDs now because in most laptops, actually most MacBooks, you are unable to play CDs anymore.

I ask the guy working if he can play the second song, and he said that it feels like this song, *The Reason* is becoming this generation's *Wonderwall*. I disagree with him, because I never really heard of this song, maybe for baby American millennials not for us.

The song kept repeating the line, 'a reason to start over new, and the reason is you'. That at least got me looking at the letter and smiling.

I look back at the words with a smile, staring at her cursive handwriting, the words flashing clear as I run my fingers over the page. I take another heavy breath. I open the letter and decide to read it.

LETTER 0
February 21, 2015
Dear Al,

We are people, who feel lost and we have lost ourselves when we lost people we care about. I never understood why people were so quick to hide their sadness instead of accepting the reality of it. Why is being sad associated with negativity? We always try to avoid sadness, by shushing wailing babies or by telling young children to not be sad and to stop crying. We tend to pass on the message that sadness is bad, that it can lead to sickness, depression, and therefore it should be avoided, when in fact sadness is an understandable expression of an emotion that reflects a feeling of loss, grief, and disappointment caused by series of events. To overcome permanent sadness and sorrow, a person should avoid getting sucked into a tornado of sadness and instead think deeply and start questioning the cause of this emotion to make better sense of these negative memories causing this confusion.

Emotions are feelings and moods that shape our interests, personalities, and how we view the world. Sadness is an emotion that can be mistaken for rocks that are tied to my feet pulling me down to drown. In fact, these rocks are my tangled memories which can be understood and arranged so that I can step on them to rise up instead of drowning. Different emotions, including sadness, can be expressed through a form of art. Running your fingers lightly over the keys of the piano, or playing the guitar, or hitting the drums with two wooden sticks as the loud sounds echo. Maybe standing on your bed or on stage holding a hairbrush or a microphone singing. Sketching a person, object, place, or maybe nothingness with your pencil. Maybe later, you would want to add colour to your sketches or simply start painting without a sketch as a guideline. You can be doing something you are passionate about, such as writing poetry, or even a piece of writing full of feelings.

I express my sadness by writing because it makes me feel alive with emotion. However, sometimes we are encouraged to conceal these emotions, as being emotional is considered being dramatic, which pressurises me to try to fit into this society as that is the way to be considered normal. This made me ignore these memories, but at the end of the day, sadness can be neither avoided nor escaped from because it is just a feeling, and accepting this feeling for what it is can help me better understand and express myself through different forms of art.

I choose to write. Writing can organise your thoughts and make you feel that things will be okay, that everything follows a certain flow that cannot be changed. I know writing while you are sad won't make you happy because happiness is not a destination; it is a state of mind, a feeling that will pass, or a mood that a person experiences. Happiness is not a place or a person; it is more complex than these simple things. Happiness is a feeling, a temporary one. Sadness doesn't mean that a person has depression because a person can experience different moods and feelings during a day; such as the feeling of happiness, sadness, anger, love, tiredness, or even excitement.

These different moods come in different orders and can either take half a day or just seconds of your day, it is just a random algorithm of feelings that are not consistent.

Sometimes a person might want to change a mood by wishing for things in life to change or happen differently. We wish we had time machines to go back in time and fix things or simply stop things from happening. There is a vivid memory that reminds me that wishes can sometimes come true. Back when I was in fifth grade. I had a purple spongy diary covered with golden stars that I got from the library. In this diary, I decided to write about what I did every day, the people I missed, and things that made me angry. In one of its light pink pages, I wrote about how much I missed my closest friend who had moved to another school. A few days later, I participated in a national day event in the airport with a group of students from the school. I was looking down making sure that I did not forget anything. When I looked up, I saw my closest friend, with her long-braided hair and glasses there, surprising me with a warm hug. Since I cannot get this memory out of my head, while writing this an epiphany hits me. Wishes can come true. Things can turn out the way I want them to. If I have a wish, I will place it in my heart, anything and everything I want. Things might turn out the way I want them to be.

I have to remember and remind you too, that the world is full of magic, and the next miracle might be in the corner of our lives. Even if my wishes might seem impossible to me like bringing people who died back to life, or bringing people who left back to me. My wishes will still come true but not in the way I want them to. I can get rid of the negativity that these memories carry by understanding myself and believing in myself. Sometimes I want to travel back in time to relive some of the good memories and avoid the negative ones. I want to go back in time to stop the negative memories from existing. I know one thing and it is that I don't have a time machine.

The years are passing, the heavy weights are still there, but they come less frequently. These different memories are from different times in my life before I experienced loss, and I am writing to understand when it all changed or when I believe it all changed. I am writing to deeply understand why we lose people. I don't want to be stuck in the past, instead I want to let go of the sadness that these memories bring back. I don't want to forget these memories because they shaped who I am today, but I want to be able to look at them and feel like they aren't heavyweights anymore. To let go of this sadness I need to overcome the fear of loss. I don't believe that writing about it can change the way I think about what happened, but if I don't write about it, I may forget the good memories that came before I lost these people. Instead, I would only recall the sadness that these memories carry.

Every memory will slowly drift away, and I will still not be able to understand why we lose people. We don't just lose people; we also lose the memory of them. First, as small details, then as parts, and one day we are left with nothing but sadness because 'time' will make me forget the good memories. Maybe I will not forget the people, but I will forget how they once made me feel. Memories can make us wish that life has some guidelines, like formulas. Just like when you solve some mathematical problem. Finding the right solution is much easier when you have the formulas. Life is not like mathematics; we cannot always predict the outcomes of our actions. We might not be able to make people stay longer in our lives. Even though sometimes all we want is a second chance to react differently to a situation, or an explanation of why certain things happen in life. It is important to let go of the sadness that comes with certain memories and not overthink the situation.

Therefore, closure is important because it makes us move on. I always feel like I am talking to a wall every time I want to say something to people who are gone, and all I hear is my own echo. My echo changes as years pass. It brings with it different excuses, different reasons why people are gone. I tell myself:

'Everyone dies, I will die one day.
Maybe something is wrong with me.
Maybe I lost everything.
What is everything?
I am very confused. I want to understand.
Maybe things will get worse.
What is the purpose of existing?
People always leave.
I've got to let it all go.'

I tried digging deep into understanding why we lose people, and, when I do, I start questioning my existence… or not just my existence but also the existence of the human species. We strive as human beings to give our existence meaning. We often ask questions like 'why are we here?', 'Do we matter or have there been so many people on earth that lived and died that our existence doesn't matter at all?', and we wonder whether we should not question our existence because it is beyond reason. These questions make me feel like I am nothing, just a trifle in this world; but we really are so little, a small factor in the world since there are millions of people breathing, millions who stopped breathing, and millions that just grasped their first breath.

We tend to look at the bigger picture rather than digging deeper. In school, they first tell you that we are made of cells, and then they tell you that these cells are made of things that are even smaller than the cell, that makes both living and non-living things. These small things are atoms, and these atoms are so small that they seem like they are nothing, but when millions of atoms are together they make a cell, and different cells can make a tissue. Tissues can make a body part and so on until the final result is our body. This same atom can be used to make the page you are reading from.

I might feel like I am a small factor, but we are all small factors. As small factors, we can cause small changes that cause a series of actions that can affect larger complex systems. Just like when you change one number in a mathematical formula, this change can cause the solution or the outcome of the mathematical formula to change. The concept is known as 'the butterfly effect'. It was attributed to the famous mathematician Edward Lorenz. Chaos theory suggests that we are often completely unaware of the impact of our actions. It is also a reminder of the delicate balancing act that we perform daily without realising it, not taking the time to realise that our words, moods, and behaviours can impact the people with whom we come in contact. Simple actions can create major results. We can't anticipate the ripples of actions, but we can still flap our wings like a butterfly knowing that our actions can cause a storm of activity.

History is full of small events that lead to big events. Maybe we all once did something that started a chain of events and might have led to the next big revolution or a huge invention that can affect our world. We are the centre of networks making us more important than we think. We meet thousands of people in the course of our life. The people we meet will also meet thousands of people making a simple action that we take each day creating a vibration in our circle. That is why I believe we matter in this world. But if we matter so much then why do we die? Why do we lose things and people we love? To understand why we die I need to understand why we are alive? Coping with loss is hard. It might be easier if the people don't really matter, but it is hard if those people mean the world to us. We all want to understand why people leave, die or go away.

The reasons for feeling low or demoralised, touch more or less everyone. We all go through things in life and no one's life is perfect. We all know that life is not perfect, and even a simple scene of young kids playing makes us ponder how little they know about life and how, as they grow older, they are going to suffer. We don't know when they will suffer but we know for sure that they will, because it is part of living. Life always has to come with suffering. When we feel lost or are losing something, we sometimes end up losing ourselves. We lose hope when we cannot take the sorrow anymore. It seems that to live through life we have to walk through a battlefield, where pointy sharp arrows are being thrown at us, but we have no shield to protect us. We feel weak at first. However, as time passes by, the pain becomes less of a hassle and more bearable because it is now part of us. It becomes easier because you turn those arrows into a shield, and you make a stronger shield from sharper arrows throughout your lifetime. I go back to look at these heavy rocks on my chest, the rocks that are tied to my feet pulling me to drown, the arrows that have been thrown at me by life, and I choose to face them. I choose to turn all these negative memories into something that can help me evolve as a person and better understand the purpose of my existence.

I lean on the window as I read the letter. I feel the cold window on my back, becoming colder as I finish reading. It has started raining but I didn't notice because I was so focused on reading. I never liked the rain; it is like the sky is crying. I remember back when we were in high school, and it rained. We would all go outside to get soaked as the rain brought us showers of happiness and joy. It made us feel like it is okay to run away from classes to feel joy.

I try to play with my memories, even digging up the rusty ones, and trying to polish them to remember how it all once was. But I am unfortunate; all the memories that I can think of right now will not shine. I come to the conclusion that my life has turned colourless. I grew up in the sea and change was unbearable. Then I lost the sea and change was inevitable. I am surrounded by skyscrapers that are holding onto the clouds. Time zones are constantly changing and landscapes are just dull green paintings. I fear pain but I crave excitement. I feel alone but I am comfortable on my own. When you walked into my life, all my senses were awakened. And again, when you were gone, everything became numb, and anger remains. I blame it on God, as I leave the café and the showers of the holy spit pour on my head. The rain reminds me that I am incapable of grasping anything. I was a constant chaser, but as I got closer, everything got further away. I press against the window as I peruse the letter, the chill of the glass becoming icier with each sentence. Rain has begun to fall, but I'm oblivious, engrossed in my reading. Rain, to me, resembles the sky's tears—melancholic and bittersweet. Recollections from our high school days surface, a time when rain meant liberation and happiness—a chance to escape classes and embrace joy. I attempt to resurrect my memories, even the rusty ones, buffing them until they shine anew. Yet, my endeavors seem cursed; the memories remain dim. It strikes me that life has drained of color. I was reared by the sea, where change was insufferable, then, suddenly, the sea vanished, and change became my only constant. Skyscrapers cradle clouds, time zones shift, landscapes blur into dull canvases. I'm caught between fearing pain and yearning for excitement. Alone, yet comfortable. When you entered my life, senses ignited. In your absence, numbness ensued, resentment lingered. I point to the heavens, blaming a higher power, leaving the café, rain's sanctified drizzle baptizing me.

Raindrops mirror olden days, evaporating on the sidewalk's bricks. Am I heartless? Numbness envelopes me, yet tears flow, sprinting like marathon runners. I toy with a bead bracelet, which fractures silently, its pieces scattering. There's nothing to shatter, to break into smaller fragments. I grope for the beads, but they slip through my fingers, surrendered to the rain's rhythm, sinking toward a distant drain. Let them be, deception evaded, no need for them to shatter again. I'm not sorrowful, I insist, an emotion eludes me. I inhabit a neutral realm, a space between happiness and sadness—a vast emptiness. I'm engulfed in grayness. Advice rains down, like mournful voices: "Everything has a purpose." "Pray more; God is great." "Move on, forget." "You're young, another love awaits." Words fall flat, impotent. It's as if I've died. These letters, meant to enliven, merely ensnare me. My anticipation morphs into disappointment, the letters evoking detached narration, as if from an ancient figure. I believed they'd infuse vibrancy into memories, summon her essence. Instead, they're tangled threads—obscure words tightening like a noose. Anticipations dashed, the letters are insipid, far from the passionate love story I envisioned. It's a woman on a bare stage, a story sans end. I decipher letters from a stranger, an incongruity in the symphony of life. Is there even a rationale to this? An enigma unfolding beyond logical comprehension.

False Memories

Trapped in flesh, I'm a soul ensnared. Her audacity to provoke such sentiments infuriates me. How could she subject me to this existence? I relish control, but she defied me, moving forward as I languish. Wrath consumes me; she's permitted this anguish. My life halted, every day agony. We were destined to unite, to study side by side, a childhood pact we nurtured. Yet, she chose the US, while I ventured to Germany. Our paths diverged, her departure dismissing my significance. I remember the last conversation we had before graduating from high school.

"So… Al how do you expect your life to be in ten years?"

"Hmm, we will be around 26?"

"Yes. I feel old already," she said.

"I want to start a business, a diamond business. They have a high value, and I can make loads of money really fast."

I really wanted to do that. She didn't say anything so I asked her where she saw herself being.

"I want my life to become more magical. I want to travel the world with you. Even if we do not travel, my world will remain magical as I look into your eyes and I see everything I want in this life. I see the stars and the moon. My heart beats faster when I see you smile while you are looking into my eyes, your beautiful eyes."

"Okay. So, you want to write?" I knew her well.

She smiled.

"I hate what I write, the words are just not connected," she replied.

"What do you mean?" I asked.

"I cannot write like the good writers," she said.

"You do not need to write like them," I said.

"I do not even speak good English, well that is what the girl told me in class. She threw the story that I wrote in the trash and said this is where it belongs," she said.

"Maybe your writing is not ready yet," I said sincerely.

"What do you mean?"

"You need to improve your English to write better," I responded.

"Al… You never read anything I write, how can you judge my writing without even reading it. I really had a bad day and all I needed was some support," she replied.

I didn't know what to say. I had never bothered to read any of her writings but I didn't know if she wanted to share them. I feel empty and it is becoming normal. If I could rewind time to that specific moment, I wouldn't have blocked her. Why did I even do that?

Reading the letter has stirred up forgotten memories, causing her presence to resemble a fleeting shadow. As if attempting to seize a shadow, any effort to grasp her dissipates her essence.

Deleted

I lay back down on my bed. I cannot leave the letters till the next day. I put letter zero back in the box leaving the box open. I pick letter 1 and open it. I take a deep breath and start reading.

LETTER 1
March 15, 2012
Dear Al,

Our families are our goggles into this life at a younger age. We can certainly learn a lot from them, but they can hurt you too in ways that you cannot explain to anyone. So you bury it inside of you and you refuse to write about it. You refuse to write a million reasons why you cannot believe in love anymore. I want to tell you but I cannot tell you now. I will tell you some other time or I might never tell you.

During middle school, my mother would drop my four brothers and me at my aunt's house to wait for the school bus, because our house was so far away and she needed to go to work on time. The school bus also dropped us back at my aunt's house so I spent most of the day there watching cartoons on the TV they had in their kitchen for a couple of hours until my mother finished work and picked us up. When my favourite cartoons were over and I had nothing else to do.

I would go to my grandfather who had been living with my aunt since my grandmother died a few years earlier.

Oboi Saeed was a man of the sea; he loved the sea because he used to go diving before he lost his eyesight. However, now someone has to go out with him if he needs to go out. The only time he didn't need anyone to assist him while walking was around the house because he had lived in it all his life and he knew every inch of it. To feel free, he would leave the house to walk around the house. I saw him when he went out and tried to observe. He would put his hands on the white drywall so as not to lose track of where he was, and then he would start counting while he was walking.

"One, two... fifty." Every time he counted till he reached the same number fifty and then it would take him another fifty to walk back. When he was done walking back and forth, then he would walk back inside.

On regular days, you would hear him singing Emirati songs about the sea that I no longer remember. I would go to 'Oboi Saeed', after I was done watching cartoons to ask him to tell me a story. The only thing that I remember of him are his stories because he repeated the same ones over and over again. He would always tell me the story of the mouse, and when I asked for more stories, he would tell the story of the magical pot.

"The story is about a mouse."

I would listen intently every time.

He would go on:

"While the mouse walks out of his home, the smell of bread makes him hungry.

The mouse walks, walks, and walks to the bakery to get some bread.

But the baker tells the mouse that he needs wood.
So the mouse walks, walks, and walks to the carpenter to get some wood.
But the carpenter tells the mouse that the wood is in a locked box and he lost the key.
So the mouse walks, walks, and walks to the key maker to make him a key.
But the key maker wants money.
So, the mouse walks, walks, and walks to a wedding to get some money.
But the bride wants milk for her kids.
So, the mouse walks, walks, and walks to the cows to get some milk but the cows want grass.
So, the mouse walks, walks, and walks up the hill to get some grass.
But the hill wants the rain to grow the grass.
The rain is in the clouds and the clouds are controlled by God."

I have heard this before, but I remember it differently; it is a famous children's song that everyone used to sing in school though we all claim that we learned it from our grandparents. My grandparents died before I was born, so my father is the one who told me about it but there was no mouse in the song. It was about a father who travelled and got his daughter a gift, but the gift was in a box, and he lost the key to the box. Therefore, he goes to the key maker and then the song continues with the same ending. This song makes me feel young again. It brings with it so many memories. I smile at the memory and continue reading.

My grandfather never explained to me the moral behind the story of the mouse because he wanted me to understand it by myself. At a young age, I thought of the stories as just stories with no meaning behind them. Just something that people make up when they are bored. I never thought that there was a moral behind it. Also, we never asked my grandfather about the moral and why he was telling us the story. We just wanted to hear the story. Now, I know after going through some losses that there might be some things that you truly want in life: a job, a loved one, or even a record of your favourite singer. You might end up doing whatever you can to get the thing you want. Trying to push yourself to the extreme. In the end, you will realise that there is a higher power controlling the things you want. That doesn't mean you can sit and wait for things to come to you. You should try hard to get what you really want, to think outside the box, but at the end of the day, don't get mad at yourself for not getting what you want.

He also told us another story about a magical pot. This magical pot was given to a poor family to provide them with food. The magical pot didn't require many ingredients to prepare food. The family just had to ask the pot to cook, and it would prepare what they wanted in seconds. This was the best gift the family would ever ask for. The poor family was getting all the food they wanted. But as time passed by, the family got greedy and started asking for more than what they needed. The pot wasn't happy with their greedy attitude and stopped working, then the family was starving again.

We are told so many stories at a young age that tell us that greed is a curse, and it is something that should be avoided. A person should actually be thankful and notice what they have instead of wishing for more but I always wondered what was wrong with wishing for more. We all want more than what we have... but maybe the story meant that we should work hard for what we really want rather than just wishing for it. However, this doesn't work in all situations, as there are things that we cannot do anything about, such as losing a sense of losing someone through death. In life, there are things that we cannot have, change, or even predict...

These letters are complete bullshit. It is like I am reading a boring book. I thought she would tell me something more meaningful but instead, she is just blabbing about some old tales. Then she starts saying I actually want to hear but crosses it out. Why isn't this like a fucking movie; why isn't she saying what I need to hear? I thought reading these stupid letters would make me feel something. I only feel absolutely ridiculous. I only hate her more than ever. I hate the way she is suffocating my head all the time. She is there all the damn time. Why is she still in my head? Get out! Why do I still think of you? Why is she so relevant? I want her to get out of my head. What happened to you when you were asleep why did you cross that part?

Vibrations

MEDYA

When I think of Al, which I do quite often. I smile because it feels like a light in my heart glows a little. No matter how heartbroken I once felt. I am happy that he has been part of my journey. He completed me from afar. He pissed me off a lot and that made me work harder. I wish him well. He is that stranger that touched my heart in some way. I will probably not love someone again in the same childish, pure manner the way I loved him. But my heart is big and I am capable of falling in love again. It took me a while to cope with the feeling of just wanting to hug him because I thought that maybe if I just gave him that one hug, he would have felt my heartbeat, and it could maybe soften things.

Leaving him alone was hard. He does live rent-free in my head, and I am not sure when I will be ready to let his shadow go. The ideal shadow I created of him was always there for me. Even when I was just a crush to him. But I forgive him, and I forgive myself for not knowing how to live alone. He is a lost soul. I am incapable of hating him. I can get angry and hate him for a little but I would always fall back to the trap. I always wished that there would be some sort of divine miracle that would trap us and force us to speak to one another. That just for once we would not be those bulls fighting one another.

He never did anything. Not one action to show me he cared. The only thing he did was run away and I chased because I didn't believe in miracles. I got pushed away every time and so I chose to stop the chase.

I chose someone else. Well, he chose me. Although we speak different love languages, and our frequencies are not the same. Yet, he would always get me some ice cream when I was down. Green smoothies when I was working. He would read the things I wrote, he would brush my hair. Kiss my forehead, and tell me how amazing I am. Even when I wanted to run away, he would stop me and tell me that he would do anything to make me happy. He would do anything to make me smile. He knew all my flaws, and he knows how I feel about Al. Yes, sometimes it annoys him because he just wants me to be able to love him the same way. He wanted us to be a team. We are very different and maybe not the perfect match. I was tired of chasing Al because the more I chased, the further away Al was. Someone else taught me how to love. Someone else taught me how to be loved. Someone else was not afraid of my sadness. Someone else was the person I will always say yes to.

Someone will make me happy.

But for now.

That's all I have.

AL

I wake up from a weird dream, surrounded by all her letters. I don't remember falling asleep. I think I was moving a lot while I was sleeping and some of them are crumpled up all over the bed. I should have left the box on the table. I place letter two in my bag and rush to work.

I expect my boss to get angry at me for being late again. I remember this guy from the office, Steve, who got fired for being late. You know how there is this person in every office, and no one knows their name. So, everyone assumes his name is Steve. So yeah, Steve got fired. If I am late, I will be the next Steve and I will get fired. It is not a good time to get fired, if I got fired then I would have to go back to Dubai and, at this point, it is the last thing that I would want to happen. It is very hard to find jobs, and if I get fired, I will have to look for another job.

I never thought my life would turn out like this, I never thought I would be under anyone. I thought I would be successful, and I would own my own business. My life didn't turn out the way I wanted it to, now I am in an office, scared of getting fired. I lost the person I love; I have lost my passion for living. I guess I have lost myself. Every day is turning into a meaningless routine. I thought moving away from Dubai might help me break that routine, but my life in New York is also turning into a routine. Everything bores me.

It is still raining and I forgot my umbrella. I go back to the room, grab my umbrella and rush to work. Nowadays, I do not pay attention to anything but my thoughts. I am losing my concentration, but I don't care to notice anything anyway. I do not remember the path I take from work to home anymore. It just feels like I close my eyes and when I open my eyes, I find myself in the office. Maybe it is because I am used to listening to music, and I drain myself into my thoughts. I feel like a machine with saved instructions that I follow, just doing things without feeling anything. Nothing makes me happy; then I am already in the office.

I am sitting in a wooden cubicle with a computer in front of me. While I am going over the documents, I see a face coming from the side; it is my co-worker, Adam.

"Hey, Al, the boss sent out an email to a dinner event that we all have to attend. He just wanted me to tell you to RSVP as soon as possible."

"Sure... Thanks," I reply.

I already know about the event, but I didn't want to go, since a lot of people will be going. But yeah, I will go since my boss wants me to. I try working but it is just so hard to concentrate when all I can think about is what the other letters might say.

One Hand, Five Dollars

It is night-time in Manhattan, and I am walking back home from dinner. I start to hear some Arabic music playing, which makes me pause for a second. It is Egyptian, and I weirdly think that I know the song. It is like I am walking down Sharm El-Sheikh or something. Is my life suddenly turning into an Egyptian movie? Anyway, I see this woman sitting outside a ten-floor building on a white steel chair next to a table that has a stereo. It is playing the song that caught my attention. I finally figured out what the song is. It is *Qareat El Fengan*, by Abdel Halim Hafez. Next to her is a dark purple sign that says: 'Psychic… Get your reading for only $5. Learn more about your love, career, past and the future.' The $5 sign was in bold compared to the rest of the words on the sign. The sign also had a palm with astrology signs on them. The purple psychic sign in the room behind her feels like it is calling me, like a blinking eye. The woman sitting outside looks like a gypsy; she is wearing a simple black dress covering her shoulders and a red fabric holding her hair in a bun. She has red lipstick on, and looks like she is in her late forties. Anyway, should I get a reading? I mean it is just five dollars.

Suraya: Hello there, would you want to get a reading?

I don't reply to her, instead, I just continue walking.

I can feel her behind me as I walk further; she increases the volume of the song on a weird part that says you will search for her, my son, in every place, and you will ask the waves of the sea and the turquoise on the shores about her. You will wander seas and your tears will... I don't know but I just start walking back. A few seconds later, I see myself sitting in front of that shady woman. Did she use some witchcraft to drag me to this chair? I have no idea.

I continue listening to the song that felt like it was speaking to me. I notice myself focusing on the words that say that I will return one day, defeated and broken, and that as the time passes, I will get to realise that I have been chasing a line of smoke. The lover that is referred to in the song doesn't have a land, or a home, or even an address. It ends with the line that it is hard to love a woman with no address, a woman that is hard to reach. Just like my lover who is hard to reach because she is no longer on earth. As the song ends, I see the woman staring at me with a smirk.

Al: This is a good song.

Suraya: So, I see you came back for a reading.

Al: Yes, I would like to get a reading. It is five dollars, right?

Suraya: Not anymore.

Al: What? Why so?

Suraya: You seem very confused and negative too. You know I can get a headache from reading your palms.

Al: Whatever, just read my palms.

Suraya: My name is Suraya, but you can call me Raya.

Al: You mean Thuraya.

Suraya: No. No. Su... raya.

Al: Okay. I will just call you Raya then.

Suraya: Do you mind if I smoke? I am already getting a headache from you.

Al: Okay. Can we just start the reading?

Suraya: Okay. Show me your palms or would you want a card reading that is clearer about your life. Also, if you want to ask about anyone specific, or if you want clarity with any specific situation, just tell me.

Al: I will get a card reading then.

Suraya: We need to go inside for the card reading. You do not want people's energies to mix with yours and affect your readings.

Al: Okay, whatever. Let's just get this over with.

Suraya: Okay. Come inside.

Al: What are you doing?

Suraya: I am using this sage to clear out the negative energy, and influences that are also negative that could possibly speak through the tarot cards.

Al: I see.

Suraya: I want you to hold the cards and mix them together. Then I want you to divide them into two patches. Then put the patches on the table.

Al: Okay.

Suraya: No. No. Not like that, turn them so you do not see the pictures on the cards. If you see the cards then the reading will be biased.

Al: Okay. I am getting a hold of it.

Suraya: Okay… Now choose one of the piles.

Al: The one on the left.

Suraya: Okay let me see… Oh, you got the five of pentacles. You see in this card two people walking through the icy wind and snow as they are both in poverty. One man is injured and on crutches. It says that you lack a mind-set; all you can see is what is going wrong in your life. To shift this, look for very small things that might seem insignificant and express your gratitude for these blessings. Oh my God, Al, you are grieving a big loss in your life. It is not clear whether it is in your career, love, or just life in general. But you seem wounded really bad.

Al: What else?

Suraya: I see the next card is the three of swords; it is three swords all stabbing the same heart. Your pain is something to do with love.

Suraya: The next card is one of the major cards in the deck.

Al: I see that 'death' is written on the card.

Suraya: Listen, so it might not necessarily mean death. Did your lover leave you or did something bad happen to her?

Al: Well, she died.

Suraya: Oh, this card makes a lot of sense. Now I can add up all the cards; you are in pain and wounded… and it is all in your heart. Because your woman died.

Al: Well, yes.

Suraya: The next card is the…

Al: You don't need to tell me the name of the card, just tell me what it means. I do not want to spend all day here.

Suraya: Stubborn man, naïve… very naïve. Arrogant… Why do you act like you are from the royal family?

Al: I am not.

Suraya: Elizabeth's son. I see.

Al: Haha. It is not funny. I thought you were a psychic, not a comedian.

Suraya: You think you are better than everyone, but we all know that you only love yourself and you do things only for yourself. Did you even love your wife or was she just like any of the furniture in your house?

Al: Don't you dare say that about me. I am not selfish.

Suraya: Well. I see you got the fool card, and it the first card of the deck. As expected, you try to fool everyone with your innocent behaviour, but you are just this immature reckless child. The apple doesn't fall too far from the tree as I see. You are just like your mother, a cheater living a lie.

Al: Don't you dare speak of my mom like that, she is from a well-known family. It is my fault for coming and speaking to a maniac whore like you.

Suraya: Hahaha, whore? Well, you need to tell your brothers to get a DNA test because Mommy has been fooling around.

Al: I am leaving you, crazy person!

Suraya: Your family, your life, and you are just a bunch of endless lies. Lie after lie after lie and then you are going to be living like that until you see the truth.

Al: Here is your money! Although you do not deserve it. Just leave me alone!

What a crazy woman! What is wrong with her. This is all lies; it cannot be true. She just got mad and wanted to mess with my head. This is all just nonsense.

False Palm

MEDYA

Do you remember this conversation from when we were younger?

I started it: "So, I have been reading this book about palm reading. Take a picture of your palm and I will tell you your future."

"The exam tomorrow is not on palm reading, stop wasting time," you responded.

"I will send you my notes in just a minute. Send me your palm first."

"Do you really believe in these things?" you asked.

"I mean think about it, Al, imagine you had a book and the book could tell you everything about your life. Tell me, would you read it?"

You then said, "Hmm, what would the point of reading the book be?"

"You could know what was going to happen next so that you wouldn't have to worry about the future."

"I guess I might read it. How about you?" you responded.

"I would pick a random page and read it. If it was good, then I would continue reading."

"So will you send me the notes or should I ask someone else?" you said that.

"Fine, here you go."

"Thanks."

"Where is your palm? Come on!"

"Hmmm, okay, here... I've taken a photo of my right hand," and then sent her a picture of my palm.

"Hmmm... interesting. I see something good."

"Finally, something good."

"Yes. So, do you want me to tell you your future?"

"Hahaha tell me. Where will I be in five years?"

"Your career line looks like you will be very successful. You will marry one woman and have four kids. You will become a successful well-known artist like you always wanted. Also, you will be very happy."

"Okay, that is good."

"Yeah, it is."

"So, I think that I can see the future now."

"A book turned you into a crazy witch, yeah, right."

"You are annoying. Shush..."

"Witch."

AL

These texts play in my head over and over again. I wonder every time. Where is the life that I was promised? Nothing turned out as you said it would.

Grandpa

LETTER 2
March 24, 2012
Dear Al,
I am a person who lost herself when I lost people I care about.

I am too. Believe me when I say this.

If you can, listen to this song 'Damien Rice – 9 Crimes' while reading. I want to tell you more about my grandfather Oboi Saeed. After his brother's death, he started losing his memory. He no longer remembers where the bathroom is. He has forgotten our names, and he barely talks to anyone anymore. He is usually in his room sleeping, and, whenever I talk to him, he always thinks I am my aunt 'Meera' or 'Farah'. He still thinks that my aunts live with him even though they got married and they live with their husbands. When a person loses his memory, he loses part of himself, part of his identity. It makes me feel sad that I am not doing enough to help him. He no longer remembers those stories he used to tell me and my cousins. Those tales are lost because they are not written down. Nowadays, when I go and ask him to tell me the stories, he doesn't remember any of them.
    "Grandfather, can you tell me the story of the mouse?"

Oboi Saeed: "Which story? I cannot remember…"

Reem: "I heard that blueberries could help with memory loss, so I bought some blueberries for you, Oboi."

Those stories are the stories that I remember. When I asked my grandmother about the story of the mouse, she gave me a completely different one; one of them was about a guy who is trying to cook something that he needed some wood to cook. I asked again if she remembers the story of the mouse and she said, "What story? I don't think there was a story about a mouse."

I asked all my cousins to make sure that the stories were real, and I am not just confused; they all remembered different stories. No one remembers the exact same story. Time has made us forget the details of these stories; we remember simple details but not the moral behind them.

As a kid, when I first knew that my grandfather had lost his sight, I always wondered how it would feel to be blind. One day, I walked around the house with my eyes closed, and by doing that, I realised that his hands act like his eyes. The sense of touch can help us feel if something is cold, hot, soft, or even rough, but the sense of touch is hard to use alone without the sense of sight because sight is the most far reaching of all the senses. I always wondered how it would feel if he got his eyesight back. But, as he has also lost his memory, are all his senses useless now? I now wonder whether, if he gets his eyesight back, will he get his memory back with it? Or would it feel like a dream, as it was the 1960s when he lost his eyesight, and now he is in 2012? What would he feel like when he looked at his country and realised that it is no longer a desert? I have always wondered, but this time, if he opens his eyes, he will not remember the past.

I don't know why I am telling you this, but it feels good when I tell somebody. This is somehow connected to you, but I do not know how. Maybe I can tell you what happened after that, and it will all make sense. It might make sense to why I am telling these stories to you.
But now is not the time. I'll write again.
Till then, Love, MED.

AL

She never told me about her grandfather. The more I read the more I realise that we barely knew anything about each other. I had these letters, the key to what is causing her to feel down, but I never opened them because I thought they were about me. There was so much in her head, but I never knew about it. I want to know more about what she has not written. I wish she was comfortable enough to open up to me. Why did she keep it all in?

I lie in bed with my thoughts feeling heavy. It is like an elephant sitting on my chest and it is getting heavier and heavier. It is making me feel like the bed mattress is about to touch the floor because of how heavy I am on that bed. I can feel my breath getting heavier too. My thoughts play everything repeatedly. I am losing my mind. I cry, as I feel like my chest is about to burst. My words to her are drowning me. I start breathing faster, as my face starts turning red. I cannot move. I take my phone and google my symptoms. Maybe there is someone else who has experienced this indescribable feeling of heaviness. Maybe there is someone out there who is as confused as me.

What if I caused her death because I was just not the right person for her, what if I wasn't a good match. A glitch in the universe making us meet when we were never supposed to meet. What if all that I have caused is destruction and chaos. Every word played over and over, one after the other causing hurt and pain, the only two things that I was able to provide. I was good to her, do not get me wrong, it was just that she felt too much; she was like a sponge absorbing negativity, and that negativity is what caused her to drown. I did everything right, but she kept things in.

What Should Have?

I went into a temple for the first time. Even though I reject most of the religious things I can't help but feel for all those people that come here lost or in pain, guilt, looking for clarity. It kind of fascinates me how a single place can join so much pain and happiness for so many generations.

I remember when…
Bing Bing Bing
A text from my mother interrupts my thoughts.
"Son… It was embarrassing to face people who were asking why you weren't there for your brother's wedding."

She is disappointed in me because I didn't go to my brother's wedding, which was a few days ago. My brother called me five times but I just didn't say anything to him. The marriage is a scam. He was dating a woman for five years, left her, dated another woman, then went back to the first woman. Only to marry the woman he dated in between only months after breaking up with the first woman. The whole thing is a joke, and he only married the one in between because she might be pregnant. We will know in few months.

I couldn't go back home and listen to my mother trying to ambush me with the marriage topic. Telling me to marry a family friend, so that I do not end up like my brother. She will keep on saying how they are all married, and I am just wasting my time now.

"My friend, Anoud, has the perfect daughter for you. She is very pretty, and very rich; she will be the perfect fit for you."

My mother's orchestration of familial connections as transactions—a daughter "perfect" in looks and wealth, positioned as a fitting match—elicits my resistance. The currency of marriage becomes entangled with money, status, and wealth, reducing a potential partnership to a business deal. This is a path I'm unwilling to tread, driven by my desire to evade the uncertainty that cloaks my brother's choices, to navigate a course free from the whims of external influence.

Reflecting on the vastness of humanity's growth, from a sparse two million to an overwhelming eight billion, I grapple with the notion of soulmates lost within this sea of souls. How does fate navigate amidst such expansive randomness? The thought of ending up with the wrong person looms, a reminder that we're minuscule beings tasked with monumental decisions. Amidst my musings, a sense of clarity emerges—these are the scattered fragments of thought that assemble my unique perspective on existence.

Faded Feelings

LETTER 3
2012.
Hi Al,

I discovered a new artist. His music is so heart-warming. His name is José Gonzalez. I am writing this letter on my bedroom floor. I usually write on my desk but right now, I prefer writing on the floor. I am listening to the song 'Heartbeat' by José Gonzalez. The first lines of the song are:

'One night to be confused…
One night just speed up truth…
We had a promise made…'

Al, it has been a year since we last talked. Now everything has changed. Everything we experience in life turns into a memory that is lost after some time. Some memories are still in our heads and we do not know why, like my fifteenth birthday. I remember everything so clearly, a memory of the time before everything suddenly changed. We usually shove all the good memories, in particular, to the back of our mind and don't think of them again until we realised how it has all changed. Such a memory can bring sadness because it makes me realise that you are gone.

Thinking about these good memories, from before our lives changed, makes us dismiss them as daydreaming or thinking about nothing... so we tend not to remember good memories. But why don't we convince ourselves that perhaps remembering good memories is an inexpensive way to feel better, by feeling thankful for the good memory we had rather than thinking about how our lives changed.

So, let me recall this memory...

I remember my fifteenth birthday clearly because it was the time when I was the happiest. It was a perfect moment. On the morning of my birthday, I entered the school bus and heard everyone singing me 'Happy Birthday'. When I reached school, I walked down the school hallway and I heard birthday wishes and got hugs from all my friends. During the break hour, I remember my friend, Shahad, walking with me to the school's canteen and then said, "Oops I forgot my lunch box, I will have to go back to get it from the class." Luckily, we were close to the classroom so I walked back with her. When she opened the door, everyone started singing 'Happy Birthday' again. There were also truffles with my name on, and a cake. The cake had Kurt Cobain on it. I was so happy that I put my hands close to my mouth and start screaming! "Oh my God!" I was looking around as my eyes filled with happiness, I was surrounded by people who cared about me. They looked at me and felt so happy. I was so happy that I carried that balloons that said '16' back home but, as I went out of the administration door, the kids walked past me and pulled the balloons, letting the balloons fly into the beautiful sky. But yeah, whatever, I also got cute red roses from my friend, Shaima.

With all this excitement and happiness, I reached home and saw my stepfather in the living room. I couldn't wait to tell him everything. I was calling my mother to tell both of them about my day at the same time. When my mother came from the kitchen to the living room.

I said, "Today was amazing! My friends…"

My mom interrupted, as always, and said, "Go to your room change your clothes and then come and talk."

I didn't listen to her and continued talking, as my stepfather was intently listening to me, but my mother wanted me to change my clothes first.

"Fine… ugh."

I walked upstairs, and wondered whether it would kill them if they just listened to me for a little longer. I opened my room, and saw a cake and a lot of gifts on the bed, which made me start screaming again.

"Oh my God! Mom!"

When we live through good experiences, we start taking a lot of pictures, to help us focus more on our memories. But in fact that day I didn't take pictures, because I believed that we don't need anything technical; there is a camera in our minds already that is not controlled by us, because it is always on. It takes videos, and pictures of everything we see. It is even better than a camera because it can record not just sound and image, but also scents and stories. These memories are vivid in our heads waiting for us to remember them. Going on a memory journey, can help us to remember the experiences that didn't disappear. By simply closing our eyes we can travel back in time to remember all the experiences from our past that shaped who we are today. My family came to my room and started singing me 'Happy Birthday'. I was so happy because I had been surprised twice in one day. I looked at my family, and felt their love for me.

I don't know how to tell people that things will be okay. One of my cousins passed away when I was younger, but I didn't know how to react to my friend's aunt's death. It is some kind of magic to be able to understand someone. I was just afraid of saying something stupid. But now I am older, I know that the best way to deal with a situation like this is to go to the person, sit with them, hug them, don't just tell them it will be okay. Instead tell them that you will be there for them. Sometimes when we are lost, all we need is to feel love and support. Sadly, we will never know how losing someone feels like until we have experienced it ourselves.

Once, I was sitting in class and a girl named Mahra was sitting behind me. She got called by one of the teachers who knocked on our class door. The teacher asked Mahra to come to the principal's office because her parents were on the phone and they needed to tell her something. Mahra went to talk to her parents and, when she came back, she was crying because her aunt had passed away from cancer. I looked at her that day and didn't say anything because I was too scared to admit that I didn't know how she felt. It was during math class and we kept staring at the clock waiting for the class to end. When it did, my other classmates went to Mahra to talk to her and comfort her. I thought I understood how it felt like losing someone because I was the person who would cry if a character dies in a movie. I wanted to say something but what would I have said?

"Everyone dies"? "Things will be okay"?

I didn't know what to tell her.

I thought that her aunt had cancer and death is something that we cannot control. It is like a train ride that will take all of us. Her eyes were red, and she was hurt but there was nothing I could do, or anyone could do. When something happens to someone else, we try our best to hide our pity by trying to connect with people and understand their perspective, pain, or emotions, which lead to empathy rather than sympathy. That is not easy most of the time because sometimes it requires us to connect our sympathy with another similar memory to understand what the pain actually feels like. What I had to do is tell her that she was not alone in this, and I understood how it felt, but I didn't. It was hard for me to connect it to something in myself that knew the feeling of losing someone close to me through death. I felt empathy, and the worst part about empathy is that I tried to silver line a painful situation that another person had just shared with me. My response or anyone's response about losing her aunt wouldn't have made much difference because she wouldn't really have been paying attention to what we were saying. And she would have wanted us to tell her that it would be okay in the end instead of telling her that it was okay now.

I visited my father in jail for the first time since he was taken. He became very thin, and his dark circles were contagious. I couldn't recognize him and he couldn't recognize me either.

Your words are stuck in my head… Al… you said you cannot be with me because your feelings faded. Al, how can your feelings fade? How can I stop loving you, when every night I think about how we could be in the future? Al, I know you do not see it… But I love you and I am scared of saying it. I really cannot see a future without you. How did your feelings fade…? Don't just leave… tell me how, so that I can make my feelings fade too. Are feelings that fade never real?

Chances

High school love carries a special allure, where the simplicity of gestures can resonate like boundless abundance. I called Dr Veronika last night, and I will be going to see her today. I think I need someone to digest all these draining thoughts with. It is getting out of hand, it feels like I cannot know what is true, and what is not. I feel like everything I once knew is not what I truly thought. I have gotten used to the smell of New York. I am starting to adapt to my loneliness. I just feel too many emotions, so they cancel one another until I feel nothing. My thoughts just got interrupted by a call from Ash, my best friend. She is the person I go to when I want to talk about anything. Aisha is four years older than me. Aisha would normally treat me like her younger brother. She is the person who I can always rely on and tell anything to. But right now I have been very distant and I am not sure if it is a good idea to even respond. I have been ignoring her calls for a while now. She just texted ASAP, and that's the only reason I will answer this call. I take a deep breath before I speak.

"Hey, what's up?" I answer as I pick the phone.

"Al... I have been trying to reach you for a while now," she responds, sounding worried.

"I am alright. So again, what's up?"

"So, when are you free. Mohd and I want to have you over... for dinner? We really need to speak, Al," she responded.

"I am actually in New York... I had to go."

"What do you mean you had to go?"

"For work."

"What work are you speaking of, you are on leave." She sounded angry now.

"Ash... I don't think I will be coming back anytime soon; can you just stop bugging me?"

"Couldn't you just say goodbye before you leave?"

"It is hard to say goodbye," I say, because that is how I feel.

"Al, you cannot just run away like that; we miss you here, and baby Tariq misses you too," she responded.

"Ash... I don't think I will be coming back at all."

"Al... I know you miss her. I know you are going through a lot that I cannot really understand or help you with because I don't know how it feels like you know... we want to be there for you. It is hard for you to face all of this on your own. Just come back and stay with us... I think that's for the best," Aisha responds.

"Ash..."

"Tell me, Al."

"Remember the letters?"

"The ones you told me you found?"

"Yes..."

"Yes... What did you do to them? Did you burn them as I told you?"

"Ash... I have been reading them."

"I don't know what is in those letters but, Al, promise me that you will not do anything crazy. You know what? I am going to talk to Mohd so we can leave baby Tariq with his mother and we could come to you, and at least be there. We cannot leave you in New York alone with the letters."

"Ash… there is no need to come. I will be alright"

"You promise me you will be alright?"

"Yes, Ash… Walla (I swear). I will be fine."

"What is in the letters?"

"I do not know what to tell you."

"What is in them?"

"Just words actually."

"Words of what?"

"I would say feelings written over and over again."

"How does it make you feel?"

"Don't worry I am seeing the doctor you told me about years back. Dr Veronika."

"Actually… her name was Verona… I guess you are seeing another doctor. I hope she is good."

"She seems alright. Listen, I will speak to you soon, alright?"

"Sure, take care."

I remember after we got married when I first introduced her to Ash. Aisha would tease us, and say things like, 'the young lovebirds' every time we saw them. Aisha would get so mad at both of us because we were both stubborn when it came to what we wanted in life and wouldn't express much. Aisha is a friend that I will forever care about; she has always been there for me.

I have reached the therapist's office. It has been a while since I last visited.

I look around me for a moment. Suddenly, I just know that I do not want to narrate this story anymore at this point.

Aristotle Lied

LETTER 4
December 28, 2012

My stepfather decided to take us to the movies with his son Tariq, who was staying over for a couple of days. Before leaving home, he told Hassan to make him some tea. He was sitting in the living room looking at his phone, and then suddenly we heard screams, "HELP ME!"

We went to him. He was still sitting on the couch.

Hassan: "Dad, are you okay? Dad, answer me!"

I knew something was wrong, but I didn't know what was happening. I didn't say anything and then my mother came from upstairs.

She looked at him and said: "Why isn't he replying? Call the ambulance now!"

She said that while calling the ambulance herself.

Everyone was crying, even the maid was crying. I was scared. I wasn't able to cry because I didn't want to believe it. First, it sounded like his soul was coming out and then it was very silent. The ambulance came, it was like what you see in the movies. They took out a defibrillator and installed paddles that gave a high electric current to the heart so that the heart could start beating again. They kept increasing the current as they counted. Every time, they increased the current, we hoped that maybe now his heart would respond but there was no sign of life. Seconds later, the sound of the defibrillator stopped, and all that I could hear were screams of fear coming from my family. My mother went with the ambulance that took my stepfather. The entire process was taking so long, time seemed to stop for a while. I knew that my life was going to change, but I was still hoping that maybe when the ambulance took him to the hospital he would be okay. I watched the ambulance leaving, and stayed on the front porch of the house. I stayed there with my siblings sitting, praying and begging God to make him live longer. The sun was about to set. The colour of the sky changed with my mood from bright with colours to red showing pain, and suddenly, as soon as I received the call from my mother the sky went dark. She told us that he was gone; gone forever. And she cried. We all cried in our empty yard that suddenly became full of cars of relatives coming to the funeral. In the darkness behind the house, my brother was sitting alone, crying because he was scared of what he had just seen. He had been playing video games before all of this happened and now he didn't feel like playing anymore. He was scared. I went to him that day and told him things would be okay but I was crying too. I didn't know what was supposed to happen next. How were we supposed to have a normal life again?

I wasn't able to cry during the day because I was still in shock but when the night came, I wasn't comfortable being alone because the scene of his death kept on playing again and again in my head. I was afraid of not being able to understand what was happening. Going to sleep was the hardest part. When someone dies, it feels like it is all a dream, and that when you go to sleep things will become okay. You will wake up to see the people you lost are still alive. I kept telling myself it wasn't just a bad dream, but deep inside I knew it was harsh reality pulling every spark of happiness out of my heart. When someone dies, you feel like you are nothing. I felt nothing but pain because I ended up thinking about his death. I cried until I was short of breath, and then just forced my eyes shut.

My heart is a bird that is trying to escape out of the cage that it is trapped in. Heavy teardrops from my eyes are bouncing as they reach the floor of my bedroom. My chest feels heavy and my head is spinning non-stop. I have never felt this heavy before. I lie on the bed with the letter on top of me. I wish I could rewind time and change what had already happened. What am I doing to myself? Why am I reading these letters now?

When I said my feelings had faded, I meant… ugh, I don't really know what I meant. I was just scared of getting in trouble or even getting her in trouble. I knew we both had dreams and I didn't want to destroy them. That's why I left, because the time when I had come into her life was not the right time.

I had to get up and get ready for work.

When I woke up the next day, I thought it was all just a dream but it wasn't; it was a reality that I had to accept. People were still in our house. Everyone but my stepfather. Hours later, I was surrounded by my cousins who knew how much I loved painting. They started taking out all my painting brushes to paint with me to distract me from what was really happening.

Life is full of distractions that stop you from overthinking previous situations. Our lives are not just one genre but, instead, the situations change, causing things to shift from one genre to the other. Your life can be sad but it can suddenly turn into an action movie. Everything changed when this woman came into our house during the funeral. She looked suspicious; it was the last day of the funeral and she walked around the house during lunch with two male workers. My aunt saw them, but she thought that she might be related to my stepfather, and she was trying to help with serving coffee and tea. She was the last person to leave the house at the end; before she left she pretended to sit and comfort my mother but then she tried to push my mother down the stairs. I wasn't there at that time because I was sleeping in my mother's bed. I just heard some screaming; "Get out of the house, you killed him!"

I was terrified because I didn't know what was happening. The door was locked. So I called my aunt and told her to come as fast as possible. She called all my uncles who came rushing to check what was happening. It was during New Year's Eve and all the roads were crowded so it took them some time to reach our house. The woman was still screaming at my mother, saying that she killed him. My mother started crying, I realised I was locked in the room, I knew that there might be a spare key somewhere inside. I searched and, when I found a spare key on one of the desks, I opened the door. Then I started shouting at the woman telling her to get out. Who was she to accuse us? My uncles came in and made her leave the house. When my aunt told my uncles that she had seen her walking around the house in circles, my uncles checked around the house and found out that the woman had locked all the rooms in the house and also changed all the keys. That's why she wasn't scared to push my mother down the stairs. Clearly she thought my mother was the cause of my stepfather's death. She also thought that people would assume she just fell, since no one was in the house to witness what was actually going on. But I had been there. I am glad that I was there to ruin her plan. We told the police about her, and tried to describe how she looked so that they would catch her. That day, all my uncles slept in our house to make sure that woman would not come back.

This event distracted me for a while from the main event, which was my stepfather's death. The horror of witnessing my stepfather's death turned into another fear. I was afraid of losing my mother and her baby because of that woman. Somehow, I thought that my stepfather would be born again into my new baby sister, and if my mother fell down the stairs then that baby would have been gone forever.

Although we didn't really know who the woman was, we figured out days later that she was related to my stepfather; clearly, her pain had been controlling her. She wanted to get her revenge to feel better. Her emotions were controlling her, but she wasn't the only one. When emotions control us, it makes it hard to manage our actions. The struggle with revenge is everywhere, even in fiction. Some writers, like Shakespeare, thought that revenge was as normal as the sun rising. Others, like Gandhi, argued that revenge is destructive; he said, "An eye for an eye only ends up making the whole world blind."

People who try to take revenge don't really think of the harm that it can cause. They are just angry, and they want to express this emotion and find something that feels like justice.

Releasing the emotion of anger can make a person feel better in the moment. But after this emotion is released a person will succumb to self-loathing, wondering why they did what they did. I didn't really know at that time why she behaved that way, but I learned something from the situation. When we are very happy or too sad, we are usually not aware of what is happening around us. So, someone needs to stay calm to take care of others and make sure that no one takes advantage of our sadness to hurt us.

***

Aristotle once asked: "How does it happen that thinking is sometimes followed by action and sometimes not, sometimes by motion, sometimes not?"

Learning self-control is important because it is one of the most important aspects of having a happy successful life. It is important to master yourself by having self-control, and being able to insulate yourself from other people's reaction so you can have a better impact on the world through the work that you do. Learning your own psychology can give you the power to get rid of all the negativity in your life.

It can help you feel more positive if you distinguish between the two worlds that you are living in: the inner and the outer world. The inner is the world of feelings and emotion; it is what goes on in your brain. It is powerful because we often focus mostly on the outer world rather than focusing on the inner world inside our brain.

Yes, you want to feel happy, but anything in the outer world, such as cash, can only make you happy for a temporary period. After that time is done, you will become depressed again, because happiness, sadness, love, and anger are all located in the inner world.

We always feel that we should blame outer circumstances for how we turned out to be. This leads to the belief that we are just a victim of the things that happen in the outer world. This all ties back to self-control; a person needs to improve their inner reality so they don't see themselves as a victim, and change what is in the outer world by creating a positive mind-set. It is not an easy thing to master self-control; first, you have to think of yourself as a biological entity.

I am an organism of trillions of cells that are working together in many complex ways. My body and your body both have millions of chemical and mechanical processes that are happening just so that we can breathe and think. Most importantly they enable us to exist. Your brain is a system that regulates your body so you can adjust to the things that happen in the outer world. Your brain has millions of thermostats that are working to keep you alive. Therefore, the most important thing at the end of the day is to focus on your inner self so that you can control your emotions.

No Time to Grieve

LETTER 5
January 2013
Dear Al,

The funeral only lasted for three days but people kept on visiting us. They were trying to keep us company so that we would not feel alone. Days later, people stopped mentioning my stepfather, but in our hearts, he was still alive. Will time make us forget everything? Everything feels different, even the living room. My relatives changed the furniture to make us forget how my stepfather had died. But changing the furniture didn't take away the memory, because every time I passed by the living room the scene was repeated in my head: my stepfather lying on the floor, doctors surrounding him, and everyone crying. I remembered where everyone was standing, and what they were wearing and saying. It was just a memory that I couldn't forget. I saw his soul leaving us, and I was not able to do anything about it. Some days I also wondered whether...if I had had some knowledge of what I was supposed to do, I could have stopped what was going on. But I couldn't. It was too late for me to analyse the situation that way.

There were days when I tried to escape the tough reality of his death. It has always been hard for me to understand it.

Even now, writing about it feels like broken texts that no one can understand except me. Sometimes I wonder why I am even writing about it; but believe me, writing about it has changed something in me. I learned that what had been going on was not easy at all but I am glad that I grew as a person, and wrote about it. Writing made me list the fears that lay front of me, even as I tried to overcome these fears and stop them from controlling me.

Thinking about losing someone we are used to seeing every day is hard. Fear can make us think a lot about what could have happened, what should have happened, and what might happen in the future. I found it hard to accept the fact that my stepfather had only been in our lives for two years, and now he was gone. Nothing could bring him back. I sometimes blame it on the doctors for coming late. But sometimes I think maybe time was passing really slowly in my head, and they weren't actually late. I really don't know. I mean, maybe if the ambulance had arrived sooner they could have done something. Other times I think, 'okay maybe it was his time and there was nothing that anyone could do to stop what was happening'.

Maybe my stepfather passed away, but the values he passed on to me will always stay alive. My stepfather taught me the importance of family, as they are the people who will always be there for you when you need them. They will take care of you. When they get angry at you, all what they want is the best for you. You have to dedicate some of your time to your family to give them love in return.

My stepfather was what I wanted to be like when I grew older. He always took risks, tried new things, told us lots of stories, and took us on many road trips. We all have people who are in our lives for a short period of time, but who change us profoundly. Even if my stepfather was only in my life for just a couple of years, I felt lucky that I had had the chance to learn from him. We are influenced by so many different people. We encounter different people that can affect our moods, and our actions can cause so much change in the present and future. Everyone who has ever done something nice to us or has spoken one word to encourage us to push forward has entered into the makeup of our character.

It hurts me knowing that I should've written about him sooner, because now I can barely remember most of my time with him. A lot of things happened to me after that, and I started to forget him. I didn't want to forget any more of my time with him, so I decided to write about it. Although I don't remember most of my conversations with him, I am glad that I remember the lessons behind most of his stories. I guess that is what matters after all. Not the details but the morals we learn.

When I had to go back to school, I realised that the world hadn't stopped for me to grieve. Kids were still singing in the school bus. The world was still moving, and teachers were explaining the chapters they had to explain without caring who was in class and who wasn't. They would simply mark anyone who wasn't there as absent. Students who usually sat together to chat, were still sitting in the same places to chat.

I was in my own world of grief. Nothing stopped for me to grieve my stepfather's death. After the three days of the funeral, people moved on with their lives, except us, the people who had seen my stepfather every day, because our lives changed. No one brought it up in school, except one girl who looked at me and asked me:

"How was your winter break?"

I looked at her, and said: "Uh. My stepfather died." She said sorry and walked away.

Others were confused about my grief. They thought I wasn't supposed to be attached to my stepfather because he wasn't my real father. I will always be the daughter of the man who is in jail. Only my stepfather real daughter should feel sad, not me. They thought that I wasn't supposed to stay sad because he was not blood-related to me, just a person who married my mother. My pain was irrelevant to everyone. I never felt like I have a father. He went to jail when I was only five. I still do not know for what. Some of my classmate use to make fun of me saying that he is a murder. I have few pictures of us when I was kid. I hate that I will never be able to know the truth. I tried searching it online, but I only found his name in most wanted list. I guess no one understood how close my sister and I had been to my stepfather, and how we had viewed him. The only thing people gave me in terms of sympathy was to try to find a silver lining in the situation, and to show me that it could have been worse: "But at least he is not her father."

It was hard for people to empathise with our situation. It is true that his daughter also felt sad because of her father's death, but it was important to know that people don't experience sadness the same way. I never felt surrounded by a father. I had to adult up from a very young age.

People don't take the same time experiencing grief because it is linked to how their lives have changed. It is not just a matter of coping with loss; it is also a matter of coping with change, and that can take a lot of time. Grief is like a bullet; some people can die from one bullet. Others can survive three. Grief is a process and pain is a complicated thing. Some people prefer to just ignore their pain, thinking that it's the best way to react. Grief is not a staircase that can be climbed; it is more like a rollercoaster ride. It is not predictable; it is an uneven journey. I didn't want to take this journey of grief but I was already riding the rollercoaster and I was just waiting for it to stop. What I learned is that you shouldn't wait for the world to pity you or to try to understand how it feels like because pain is a feeling inside of you that no one can feel other than you. The degree of pain experienced is different from one person to the next. Every time I complained about something, my mother would tell me that I shouldn't wait for people to make me feel better; instead I should help myself.

She would always say that because she would never help me. I sometimes feel alone in this world. I am alone in this world. I am not sure for how long I will feel this lonely.

I am okay, do not worry.

Shadows

LETTER 6
Dear Al,

The first day of school after my stepfather's death was just long and tough. I wanted it to end, and I really wanted to go home. I was one of the top students in my class, but high school was all nonsense to me. I was considering dropping out of school. The school didn't matter to me anymore, all I wanted to do was sit at home and be alone for a while. I wanted to take the journey to understand the meaning of life to be able to understand death and not be afraid of it. I was also afraid to lose you, Al, for something greater. Something that will take you away forever. I was afraid of death taking you away.

School taught us many things, like how the heart functions, cell theory, geometry, but I don't think it taught us the reason why we are alive. We never really understood how all these subjects can help us understand that. The subject I enjoyed the most was mathematics, because I believed that everything is made out of numbers so it can help you understand the beauty of life. How is that? If you stopped for a while and started thinking about coincidences. These can all be calculated; the location, time, and space leading to the right moment. Everything happens at a specific time and location that can affect others because you are taking a specific location, and the exact moment when a person can meet someone else. All kinds of other things might have happened but because you were there they did not happen. So every move you make causes a series of actions, that could have turned out differently. You are like a small cog in a machine that happens to be there because our world is like a machine. You matter for a certain time and you affect other components. Mathematics is nature's language in which it can directly communicate with us. We are numbers that were once in someone's life. There might not be a clear answer as to why we are alive but the reason we are alive is based on us. Life is a gift that is given to us and we have the choice to spend it however we want.

At the time I felt like that the right thing to do was to break my routine. I wanted to leave everything, grab a bag and leave my phone at home. I wanted to be a nomad, travel around and not get attached to anything or anyone because I thought that getting attached just weakens me. And, at the end of the day, everything is temporary, so I should leave everything behind. Although I was never able to run away physically, I was able to take journeys in the minds of great philosophers by reading their explanations of life and death.

I was reading a lot about Al Ghazali, a Muslim philosopher, who explored the meaning of life. His father died when he was young, which led him to explore the idea of death. He said that there are different kinds of people who have thought of death:

1) Ignorant people; when they remember death, they become afraid of losing the pleasures of the world.

2) Repenters also fear death because they feel like they are not ready to die yet, and they wish they could stay alive forever.

3) Wise people are those who live life to the fullest, trying to be the best version of themselves, and remaining excited to see what comes after death.

I wanted to be a wise person, I didn't want to be scared of death. Instead, I wanted to feel excited for what comes next even if we cannot guarantee there is anything, and we have no proof of what it might be. It is still a surprise that I should be excited about. I don't want to just be a wise person. I wanted to be even greater than that. I didn't want to have a preference about whether or not it is better to be alive or dead. I wanted to just live like there is a tomorrow, and there will always be a tomorrow, but I will never know what tomorrow will actually be like. Death is sudden; it is not in one's control. Why should I be afraid?

I was trying to read, while thinking, hoping, and wishing that it will help me feel stronger. I guess it was just another distraction for now…

Anood in school said her father is police officer and he said that my father was so happy to hear that my stepfather died. I just do not understand how can he be so cruel? I never want to be like him.

AL

I need a distraction from my feelings, too. My mom called yesterday, and I let out my demons. I was angry, not angry with them but I wanted to be alone. I don't think that is too much to ask for. My brother after less than a year of marriage got divorced. As expect.

I decide to go to the New York Library. In the library, I grab a book by Al Ghazali. It was weird because I do not recall the last time I entered a library or even read a book. I see a woman sitting next to me. She looks like a hippy, with a flower crown, and colourful clothes. As soon as I look at her, she looks back at me with a smile.

I need to read something other than the letters for a break. I sit in front of her as I start reading. The woman comes close to me and whispers hello.

I am confused but I say, "Hi," back.

"Do you want to get out of here and talk?"

"Talk about what?"

"Just come with me."

"Okay."

I walk outside while wondering what the woman can possibly want, but then she disappears.

Am I hallucinating now?

Coping Lies

LETTER 7
February 2013

First, we all cried, then we started seeing him in our dreams. I remember that I was still able to see his soul walking around the house with a smile. He was still there during the funeral, but after it ended he was gone. Before his soul left, he was standing next to the stairs. When I noticed him. I stopped. It was early in the morning and I was the only one downstairs. He told me something important.

He said, "I know you; you are strong and you will get through this. But please take care of your mother and your baby sister."

He had already told us before he passed away what he wanted to name the baby before they informed us of the gender. He just knew it was a boy. After he spoke to me, I tried to ask him questions before he left.

I said, "But wait. Where are you going? Are you alive? Is this a dream?"

He looked at me and smiled.

"I am still here."

Then he was gone. After that I couldn't see him anymore.

I was a little bit scared of my hallucinations, or whatever they actually were. But it didn't matter to me whether what I saw was real or not. What mattered was that they were comforting. My life wasn't the same anymore. Whenever I came home from school. I didn't see my mother in the kitchen, or my stepfather on the couch watching TV. All I saw was an empty living room. My mother would be in her room. My brothers and I walked straight to our rooms, rather than sitting in the living room. We all ate in our rooms instead of eating together. Every time I passed by the dining room, I recalled an old scene of my family sitting and having a proper lunch. I would come in and complain about high school drama. My mother would say how much she hates my complaints, while my stepfather would listen to my lame stories. Now the dining table has been empty for months. No one bothers even sitting there because now it is the most depressing place in the house.

Everyone was avoiding the living room because it was where my stepfather died. I remember trying to sit there and just forget the memory but as soon as I sat down, I would remember everything and then just start crying. It wasn't the same as I thought it would be. We all lose someone in our life and I guess people would normally feel this way. It is a normal feeling, but at the same time it wasn't because I had witnessed his soul leaving in front of me. I was afraid of losing anyone else.

When I decided to write about it, the first thing that I wanted to say to describe my life was: "Things change really fast."

After my stepfather's death, it was hard for me to cope with the changes. I believe that the worst part about that change was how I changed myself. I became an emotional person who was too afraid to upset anyone because I thought anyone could die any moment and we could lose them forever. I became more stressed and worried about the people surrounding me. I was worried about my mother, even though my mother stayed at home most of the time. I was also worried about my brothers, who were in their rooms playing online video games with their friends most of the time.

I didn't know what I had to worry about but I would pass by every time and check on them. I was also scared of routine. I thought if person just settled in and kept on doing the same thing every day, then the person would die. I also shaved my head. My mother got called to school, and I was told that what I did is not a female behaviour. Whatever!

I noticed a common trend in books that talk about the person's daily routine. After some time you will get bored of reading the same book. I thought that God was like that; when things turn into a routine then God takes their soul away. I liked my shave head, it is cool. I feel different.

I broke my daily routine with distractions. If I was not checking on people, then I was sketching. Before my stepfather passed away, I had painted often but after his death, my colourful paintings, were replaced by pencil sketches. All the colours faded from my sight, turning to grey. Everything was dull. I hated colours. I wanted things to look like those sketches. Mistakes, things that are not supposed to happen, can be erased. Anything can be erased. Paintings are harder to fix because, when you try to erase something, the colours will get mixed up, and if the colours are mixed up, the painting will turn grey. This darkness cannot be erased, so I loved my pencil. It made me think less and at the same time think more about my sketch. I don't usually choose what I want to sketch; it just comes randomly. But when you paint you have to choose what you want to paint. I wanted the way I looked at the world to change. I wanted to enjoy life and remember that not everything is permanent.

I am not the most depressive person because I like to express my thoughts. Some people might even think that I was bipolar, because of the way I used to let out my anger and sadness instead of keeping it in around people. Then there were other times when I would joke around to not feel sad.

People made me feel that it was wrong to let out my fear. They would tell me that everyone goes through things; I was not the only one and I should stop acting like I was. I already knew this but I also knew that what makes me sad is my fear. I was losing myself because I didn't know what the hell I was doing on earth. I would sit some days praying to God, asking him to help me understand what was wrong.

I was scared of being alone in my room because I would end up thinking too much. I would sit and Skype with my classmates every day and study with them instead. That is how my grades gradually increased. In school, the only thing that I looked at was the clock, waiting for time to pass. When time felt like it was moving slowly, I would grab a pen and start sketching. Random sketches that felt like they were taking me to another world. I wasn't suicidal; I was just lost. I kept on asking myself that same question. Why are we alive?

To understand death, it is important to understand why we are alive. We are born, we learn how to talk and read, we go to school, we graduate from school, we get our driving license, we go to college, we graduate from college. After graduating from college, we start working, then start a family, then we get old and then we die. Behind everything we do in life, we ask the question, why do we exist, what is life all about? Every religion has a story to explain why we are alive. Some people choose to ignore this question by having fun, but even then, when they experience sadness and grief, they still stop for a while and start questioning. The fact that we question our own existence shows that there is some truth that is untold.

When it comes to questioning our existence, the most important thing is to make logical sense of something. We want to know if our life has any meaning, but first we need to understand what it means to be 'meaningful'. Meaning comes from the fact that something references something else. If someone came to you and asked you about the meaning of a certain word you would point to another word that would point out to another word and so on. As people, we have to imagine things that could exist or that no one has seen before. If I asked you to imagine afterlife, you wouldn't imagine it the same way I would. Our imagination varies, depending on our life experiences, beliefs, personality, and how our brain works. Maybe the question doesn't even apply to us and our existence doesn't require meaning. Maybe we don't need a clear meaning for existence.

However, by searching for a meaning to our life we are reasoning about our existence with what we believe is logic. Logic is usually defined as well-structured thought that is used precisely to build a solid argument. Aristotle reduced logical thinking to a basic structure known as a syllogism. If A is B and if B is C, then A is C. We can use two pieces of information to find a third piece that is not immediately obvious to us. This only works if the first two statements are facts; then we can find a third statement that is true. However, if we are just assuming that the first two are true then we can't guarantee that the third one is also true. Therefore, when we think about the meaning of life we should not approach it from the logical perspective.

It is true that logic can help us to find a specific meaning that is based on observation and inference, another type of reasoning, but the meaning of life and death cannot follow from this. The meaning of life is not something logical that we can observe. We can believe in whatever is going to make sense to us, which is limited and cannot exceed out of the box of logic which allows for the use of syllogisms. Logic can limit our thinking into the belief that every cause must have an effect. Therefore, no matter how much we believe in this life, it is still not enough to prove anything about the afterlife, because the law of logic might not apply in the afterlife. The universe doesn't have to make sense to us because it might be irrational than we could ever wrap our minds around.

There are different religious and non-religious belief systems that give different meanings to life. For instance, Muslims believe that the purpose of this life is to secure heaven by living according to the guidelines of Islam. This life is seen as a phase, a process, a means to an end (heaven). Buddhists believe that the purpose of life is to end suffering by detaching oneself from the world, where we often hold onto things that don't last forever, which causes us to suffer. Albert Einstein thought of the highest stage of consciousness as being the highest ideal and what gives life meaning. This comes about through the ability of the mind to think and create something from nothing, which is the greatest thing that we can do. He says a person can give his life meaning by creating things he or she loves and bringing them to the world. It is up to us to follow a belief system that makes more sense to us.

It is important to overcome sadness by understanding the purpose of our existence, not just by following religion blindly. I was born in a Muslim country where people have to take Islamic studies in school but it depends on the school you go to whether you get a good teacher or not. In my high school, not only were the Islamic teachers religious but also our biology teachers would link everything to religion. One of my biology teachers explained to us how she saw Islam as being more like a lifestyle that she enjoys following. She wasn't forcing anything on us; instead she was telling us things that she truly believed in. I remember one time when I went to her and asked her, "What makes you believe in what you believe in?"

She looked at me and said, "The first word that was sent to the prophet Muhammad (peace be upon) from the Quran was 'Eqra', which means 'read'. So I believe the best way for a person to believe in the existence of God is through reading and learning more about this universe."

I respect all the religious talk but I believed in science instead. However, the idea of higher consciousness is interesting because we humans we use mostly our lower consciousness, which focuses on ourselves. When we are in a meditative state, we can access the higher mind, which includes our imagination. That is when we are able to look at the world from a less biased, more universal perspective. That is when your mind moves beyond its particular self-interests and cravings, making your emotions less important than you thought they were. When you reach a higher state of mind, your human interests are put aside and you can be one with nature: trees, mountains, clouds, or even the universe as a whole. You start hearing the sound of the waves with your thoughts and for a while you forget about human existence.

I am not saying that a person should follow a certain belief system because there is no clear absolute. There is no 100% certain belief system. We were taught to believe that there must be a reason for everything. It is sad to see how some religious people became so superficial that they follow modern scholars blindly, without digging more into understanding why. Some people even say that it is Haram to question, when in fact it is important to question in order to better understand. Past Muslim scholars such as Al Ghazali and Ibn Sina based their knowledge on thinking, observing, and reading different philosophers that had come before them. Some Muslim scholars today have instead shifted the way they view religion, as a set of obligations, meaning that the purpose of certain actions and requirements are only known by God. In fact, there is a meaning behind everything you do. I don't believe that religion should be forced on people. It should be taught to make religious people ask themselves questions, to become better believers who understand themselves better rather than superficially believing everything they hear. I don't want to be a superficial person, a copycat who would just do things because other people are doing them.

Even though most religions give different accounts of how we came to exist, the meaning of our life is still shaped by us. I want to make the most of my life by spreading positivity and dedicating myself to becoming more educated. I believe we should make the most of our life because that is all we have for now. And I believe that dying is not an end because not everything that seems like an end actually is an end. It is like being born in a different world. This world is a mother's womb and, by dying, you get out of your mother's womb. In your mother's womb, it is all and it feels like there is nothing next, but after that, you are born, and you can see that getting out of the womb wasn't the end. So dying is not the end, instead it is a mysterious 'next'. It is like the adventures my stepfather went through. Now he is in a new adventure to discover what's in the afterlife. That's what I think happens to the soul.

A person lies naked in the grave without any of the material possessions they had in life. You will leave your phone, favourite glasses and everything you worked so hard to obtain in this world. What you know for sure is what will happen to your body. After a person dies, some people bury the body, while others cremate it. But after some time the body joins nature as explained in a poem called 'Thanatopsis', by William Cullen Bryant.

> *To mix forever with the elements,*
> *To be a brother to the insensible rock*
> *And to the sluggish clod, which the rude swain*
> *Turns with his share, and treads upon. The oak*
> *Shall send his roots abroad, and pierce thy mould.*

The poem explains how buried or cremated particles of the body join the beauty of the earth, travel into the deep oceans, and up to the highest mountains and mix with the clouds. The clouds move to different places, and some of those particles will go down with the rain. Part of the body will become part of the trees, flowers, and the soil. So why should a person be afraid of death if his/her body will be part of nature. Our atoms will travel to the galaxies, step on the moon, move around the planets, and pass through black holes. The places where our body cannot travel as a whole are infinite.

Everything is structured in a complex way. The small details are not just random. Humanity has discovered things and evolved from the Stone Age just by observing nature and experimenting. Everything is beautifully made; look at the details such as the many varieties of animals and plants that have different structures with different ratios. Everything is precise and follows a certain ratio according to its purpose. Sit for a while and think of a bee; the ratio, size, and shape of the bee all make it able to fly. Humans have observed birds and created airplanes with different sizes, shapes, and ratios. The size, shape, and ratio of a plane depends on its purpose. The purpose of the bee is to carry the pollen from the flowers and for it to fly it follows a different mechanism that requires a lot of movement and sudden turns. Meanwhile the plane cannot turn suddenly, due to its fast speed compared to a bee. Everything has a purpose, even the small details are purposeful. When the stars exploded billions of years ago, the formed everything that is the world. Everything we know is stardust, as well as I am.

Sometimes we have no idea why things happen. Every time that I wondered why I kept telling myself that everything is made out of numbers, the best answer was that everything happens for a reason. There are numbers that are arranged in certain algorithms that predict the cause of events. It's just that we cannot read these algorithms and we cannot predict why certain things happen. And that too is part of the beauty of the universe.

Fake Identities

LETTER 8
Dear Al,

Listen to this song... The Script – 'Breakeven' while reading this...

Our life consists of moments from the past that we carry with us because they changed our perspective or maybe just distracted us for a while from reality. When I became friends with Mariam on social media, she was fun, she would start talking about TV shows. That's when I started telling my friends about this cool friend I had met online. She was a great distraction from reality. All we would chat about was TV shows, music, and books. I didn't even care to know if she was a real person at that time as, after my stepfather's death I really needed someone to talk to. I would go to school every day and talk to my closest friends about the TV shows that I had started watching because of Mariam.

I even made my school friends watch these TV shows with me. We all started watching One Tree Hill *and argued about who should have ended up with who and who deserved who. In that period, I didn't care about anything else in class. We would walk together every day, and sit in the same spot every day. I didn't want to think a lot about things, especially death.*

I was becoming a new person, although I was still afraid of death.

Mariam didn't talk a lot about herself, but I knew she was at my cousin's school. She was not in the same class as my cousin. I asked my cousin about her after a while to make sure she was real. My cousin told me that she was suffering from cancer. I didn't want to tell Mariam that I knew this because I thought I might show pity and that, if she actually wanted me to know, she would have told me, but she never did. I was still shocked, because her situation was worse than mine and she was acting like she was so happy. She was listening to me complaining and even crying. It made me think that happiness is not based on our situation but on our state of mind. Our suffering can make us grow, and life is all about endless growth.

Life after is full of distractions that can make us think less about death. But the fear of death came back when a 17-year-old graduate from my high school suddenly died. I didn't know him, but I had seen him once in the nurse's office. He had come to the office to get some papers. The nurse had looked at him and said, "You are going to graduate and leave us! We will miss you!"

I remember his reply clearly: "I will not leave, don't worry, I will still be visiting."

That's the only time I encountered this person. A year later, he was gone.

The Year of Death

AL

I remember him. He was my brother's best friend, and he used to come to our house to play video games with my brother. He would always pass by the Starbucks close to our house to grab us coffee. Although I was younger than him, and we didn't talk much, he was nice to me.

I remember the night he passed away clearly. I was devastated because I remember the last phone call my brother received from him. He was sitting on the couch, and his phone was next to me ringing.

Ring ring ring

"Al, get my phone… I am too lazy to get up."

I went and got his phone for him, I looked at the screen; it was his friend, Ob.

He grabbed the phone from my hand and replied right away, "What's up, fam?"

He looked at me, and said: "Yeah, Al, will be coming with us! So I will see you tomorrow… bye, Ob."

He hung up then started checking his messages.

I looked at him, confused. "Where am I going with you guys?"

"Jet skiing."

"Hmm… sure why not? When?"

"Tomorrow morning."

We packed the next day, and my brother drove us to Ob's house. We rang the bell; his parents weren't there because they were travelling. He wasn't answering his phone. My brother thought maybe he had just bailed on us. So, we went back to the house.

Time passed, and by night-time, we still hadn't heard from Ob. He didn't usually disappear on us like that. Something seemed wrong.

So we went back to his house, and tried getting into the house from one of the windows that weren't locked. We managed to open it and climb inside.

Ob's room was locked, and he wasn't answering so my brother kept knocking the door.

"Ob, open the door!" Then we saw someone walking behind us, it was Ob.

"Oh my god, what are you guys doing?" He looked confused.

My brother ran after Ob to hit him while shouting, "You scared me... I am going to hit you till you cry! Also, why did you bail on us?"

"My phone fell in the toilet, and man I was so disgusted I flushed it."

"Man, you are an idiot."

I looked at him laughing. "Did it even flush?"

"It did, I would have liked to film it since I would have got loads of views on YouTube for that video, but... yeah the only thing I could have filmed it on was gone."

My brother looked at him and said, "Let's go and get you a new phone."

We hopped into my brother's car; since I was the youngest, I sat in the back.

Ob turned on the radio. *Sorry For Party Rocking* was playing.

I hated that song; it was so loud.

My brother looked at Ob and said, "We are getting you a Nokia, until you learn to appreciate iPhones, you spoiled child."

He turned the radio down and said "No, no, no" while switching to the other channel.

The song *Timber* by Pitbull was playing.

"Listen," said Ob. "I didn't choose for the phone to fall into the toilet. I was brushing my teeth and as I walked it fell from next to me deep into the toilet. So I didn't choose for this to happen... not my fault, so I will get an iPhone."

I looked at both of them and said, "You know the new iPhone is out."

Ob said, "Yes, I am going to be getting that."

My brother parked his car next to an electronics store.

"Okay, Ob and Al, get out, get the phone, and I will be waiting here for you guys. Don't take long."

***

In the store, Ob was walking around looking when he looked at me and said, "You think I am spoiled, right?"

I looked at him and said, "Maybe sometimes."

"I hate being like that... You know, Al, you need to work hard in school. I applied to medical school in Ireland, and they didn't accept me. My father is mad. He thinks it is because I didn't work hard but it is not because of that."

"What are you going to do?"

"I will not go to medical school; I don't even want to be a doctor. I will get into the stock market and make my own money."

He grabbed one of the iPhones, and bought it with his father's credit card.

"You are a good man, Al; you know that right?"

"I guess so."

We walked back to the car, and dropped Ob back home.

A week later. He was found dead in his bed.

My brother was crying and I was crying too. My brother had to go back for his military service the next day, and I had to go to school. We had to go back to our normal lives as if there was nothing wrong happening. Grief had to stop for the world to continue, but that grief caused some destruction in us, deep down in our souls. I think it is a lie when people say time heals. It doesn't. He was only 17 when he died. That meant something to me. I was two years younger than him when I saw this. Now, I'm ten years older and he is still 17, I guess. That's crazy.

Where Were You?

LETTER 9
2013.

I remember how everyone was so sad and they were playing verses from the Quran at school. I didn't know him personally, but I was just scared of the idea of death. I felt like the angel of death was surrounding me. Death is something that doesn't know age and doesn't care about anything. I was scared and started wondering who would be next. I thought I was the only one who felt this way, but it turned out that Mahra felt the same. As I said, Mahra's aunt had passed away a few months before my stepfather's death, so she would talk to me every day in school and would often bring up the topic of death. She was afraid of it because, when people around you die, you feel like you are next and you need to prepare for dying. Thinking about how we might die next, we started apologising to all the people we had been mean to, and expressing our emotions to people we cared about.

She would say, "If something happens to me, take my phone, text the people I truly care about and tell them that things will be okay."

She would also tell us how much she loved us and how badly she didn't want to be alone. Now I understand why we felt that way but that year was hard for the two of us. We tried to forget our pain by taking care of each other. When someone would get sick, we would go to the mosque and lie down with them. Death was frightening us so we tried to distract ourselves by reading and writing to avoid overthinking. I was distracting myself but I was still unable to escape my pain.

When the Emirates literature festival arrived, we participated in the writing competition. Mahra wrote about her aunt who had passed away because she thought that letting it all out could make her feel better. At that time, I couldn't write about it, so instead I wrote about the sea. Neither of us won the competition, but it was the first time we started writing for both of us, and I fell in love with it. It was the best way for me to express my thoughts. By writing everything down I could release all the energy that was pulling me down. But it sounded like broken text because it was hard for me to let out all of my emotions. I still needed more time.

We thought that this was the end and now we should focus on what we have. We started to enjoy our high school teenage life. Mahra used to bring us food every day in the second class by telling our English literature teacher that she needed to go to the bathroom. Instead of going to the bathroom, she would go to the cafeteria to get us food. We would sit in class and eat until we were full. Other days we would secretly order from Pizza Hut and sneak the pizzas in, or else we would hide a Dalaah (vacuum flask) under the table to drink some tea with milk when our teacher was looking at the other side. We felt like we were living life on the edge, not caring about anything, and trying our best to make every day exciting and to live our lives before death came.

I don't think I ever want to visit my father. Not anytime soon. Social media was a great distraction from reality because I was able to write down all my thoughts using Twitter and watch funny people on YouTube who were just having fun and ignoring everything else. It was also a great tool for me to meet new people; through it I was able to listen to strangers' problems which made me feel like I was not the only one. There was a girl whose parents had both died in a car crash; a girl whose little brother had drowned because she got distracted while babysitting him.

We all think 'what if', but it cannot change anything. The girl who was babysitting her brother wished that she hadn't been listening to music or that it had at least been at a lower volume. The girl who lost her parents in a car crash wished that they hadn't had to leave the house that day. She wished she had stopped them rather than nagging for a new camera. They both felt like that maybe they could have done something to change what was going to happen, but there was nothing that they could do. There's nothing they can change except trying to forgive themselves. None of us know what we're going to lose, and when we're going to lose what we have. Death and loss cannot be escaped, but we're still scared because they cause us pain. We cannot change the fact that we will feel pain when we lose something we love.

Al, none of these letters are going to be about you. They are not about you because of what you did to me. I cannot share it because I do not need to remind you of what you did. You know what you did to me.

I will only write what I wish you would do…

I will write things that I wish had happened.

I wish you had told me, "I enjoy your writing, please continue with it."

But instead, you said this:

"Stop writing, your grammar sucks."

AL

I didn't say that you always do this… you twist my words and then play the victim card. Have you forgotten what you did to me? Are you really wondering why we stopped talking? Are you out of your fucking mind? You have doubts about whether I loved you, because you doubted your own value and thought you didn't deserve to be loved by someone like me. You used to think my feelings for you were merely courtesy, and my show of love was mere acting! Acting? How could you even know acting from the truth? Acting, silly woman, belongs to the cinema, the stage, the theatre, and television. We aren't in a show; this is real life you are talking about. In your whole life you weren't really a theatre person, how would you know acting? Acting, my love, is an art and a skill that is hard to obtain. It is an art about which more books have been written than the hairs on your head. That's why you shouldn't listen to your heart when it comes to this kind of thing. You went on trusting your heart until you realised where this heart of yours had got you! What is the matter with you? My problem was that I would open my heart to you, and you would not do the same. I would let you in, but you wouldn't even give me a chance to understand you. You should have sent the fucking letters, at least I would have been able to tell you my side of the story, but you kept them to yourself, because you are a selfish woman. You never open up to me, and then expect me to read your thoughts.

MEDYA

Al, you crushed me in so many ways… the problem is you never loved me as much as I loved you. I have always felt this weird connection towards you. I hate you.

The only thing you caused is destruction. You made me feel more alone than ever. I still don't know why we are strangers; but most importantly, I don't know why you have to treat me like I am worth nothing, a person with no feelings. A rock that you will constantly kick.

Al, you shared everything about my father with your friends. You shared with them my childhood trauma! Things I can never write in a letter. Everyone made fun of me for something that happened when I was subconscious. My pain was a joke to you. Al, you never thought that maybe I was grieving and trying to heal, and maybe I was attached to you because I feared being alone. Couldn't you let me heal in peace?

Al, if you were to come back to me, and I said I do not love you… you would not fight for me. I poured my heart into my writings. I know that you will never believe in me. But I still wish that one day, you would come back to me and tell me: "I am proud of you."

Could you have a drop of care in your heart to be here? I hate that I always forgive you. When I am just a doormat to you.

The Letters

AL

Do you remember this scene that needs to be in both narratives?

> MEDYA
> Which?

AL

The one about the letters.

> MEDYA
> Yes.

AL

"Let's write each other letters. Like the ones in Romeo and Juliet," you said.

I was confused: "Letters about what?"

"About anything, just before summer starts. I want it to be special."

"Okay, how long should it be?"

"It doesn't need to be very long, it can be two or three sentences. As long as you want it to be."

"How will I give it to you?"

"Hmm… you can leave it somewhere and I will collect it."

"Okay that seems like a good idea, I will do the same."

Since the seniors had a day off, their classrooms were empty. So, we hid the letters behind the pile of literature books.

I was starting to like her, but I didn't want to get attached to her. She was the first girl I had ever spoken to, the first I had developed these strange feelings for. The first to give me this hard to understand kind of spark, but everyone feels this the first time they fall in love, don't they? Or was it more than that? Isn't this supposed to come at a later time in life?

Anyway, I wrote her this long letter with a heart at the end. And she wrote one sentence. I put so much effort into it while the only thing she could write was one sentence. She couldn't write more, and you expect me to believe that she loves me. Why couldn't she write more? The letter was disappointing so I threw it away. She even made her friend write it. She couldn't write it with her own handwriting.

Summer started. One of my friends told me that she didn't really like me, and she was just playing around. She is a liar; she doesn't really love me. She uses her grieve as an excuse to stab people on their backs. One even said he saw her sitting in a cafe with another boy. Yes, I should have asked her but instead, I was mad so I screenshotted all our chats and shared them with my friends. In a society where you are not supposed to express your love and keep everything to yourself, I think I did the worst thing a person can ever do to someone they love. I was angry. Everyone was telling me that it wasn't right to be with her, but I had no excuse to hurt her. I am not a horrible person. I never meant to hurt her. I lay down on my bed and suddenly I see everything spinning, I can't move.

2014

LETTER 10
2014.

I do not know what to say but...

I messaged you, Al, you haven't talked to me in months. Have I been thinking that maybe someone took your phone and did this to me? Because when you love someone you should never hurt them, right, but you did. I do not think you did this on purpose. I made fifty million excuses as to why this happened... I was called names in school; I was afraid of walking in the hallways... I was afraid that my life would be over and that people will remember me in that way forever. I didn't know what to say to people. I just wanted to be alone, but it was out there for everyone to see. I was scared my mother would find out in which case she would probably lock me in the house.

You saw me hurt and you walked away, Al. That's what you are good at, walking away.

I texted you with good intentions, trying to lie to myself by saying, "I know it is not you." You didn't bother to respond. That day... I filled my tub with water, and I was just lying down for hours thinking how love is a lie, and how my life was coming to an end. But I guess that wasn't the worst part...

The worst part was seeing you with someone else, pretending not to know about it. From all the people, Al? From all the people you could choose you decide to date my best friend. Mai wanted me to forgive you and remain obsessed with you so she can seem normal, right? Because she is dating you, and when do I find out about this... eight months later... Eight months of me constantly trying to get in touch with you. You loved her, Al, you did and she destroyed both of us. I just saw you a few days ago looking at her, the same way you used to look at me. When I see you not looking at me the same way anymore, I know I just do not matter to you.

I see you walking to meet her in the same place we first met, I have seen all of it. You got her a necklace on her birthday. I have seen it all, Al, but you didn't know I was seeing this. What sucked, even more, is her lying to me, telling me that you miss me while she is with you. She destroyed me, and you destroyed me too. Both of you were like poison going through my veins. I go back home, and act like it is all okay. But it is not okay.

I don't want to be her. I wish you could just tell me the truth. I wish I had never fallen for you, AL... You want to know how I felt... I felt that my life was horrible, and everything was not okay. Why was I not enough for you?

AL

It wasn't like that. I did not replace you. You lied to me. Did you forget that? Did you forget all the things you made me go through? Why am I even trying to justify what it was? It was in the past; so does it really matter? Why am I even reading these letters? Why do you always make yourself seem like the victim of circumstances, and make me look like the monster who broke your heart? Did you forget how you stepped on mine?

I changed. I tried to make it right didn't you see that.

"It was right… You were the right one for me or I wouldn't have asked you to marry me. I was young and stupid before that and marrying you was never a mistake!" I shout as it echoed through the empty room and then I realise how I was talking to myself.

I am becoming crazy. I don't cry but I am crying like a child. I need to stop reading these letters, they are taking control of me.

"I loved you and I still do…"

I made it right, I married you. Isn't that enough proof that I wanted you all for myself? I wanted to make you happy, and I really thought by marrying you, you will forget it all. We were meant to be happy together. I know that she would be crying at night sometimes for no reason, I didn't say anything hurtful to her to cause the crying. Is it my fault that she was depressed? I treat her like a queen, and I provide her with everything she would need and want. I do not get why she cried some nights. Yes, I didn't bother to ask her why, but I thought she might not want to share her feelings with me. That's why I gave her the distance she needed. I tried to be the best husband she could ask for. Indeed, I was the best she could ever get. I didn't want her to leave me. Yes, I was scared of losing her, and I didn't know what to say to her when she cries. Once she stops crying, she would come to bed, and I would hug her tight and she would never tell me what just happened. She only says that she had to use the bathroom.

What was I supposed to do when there was something clearly wrong with her?

MEDYA

I have always dreamt of the perfect departing line for this story. I wrote hundreds of possible endings until I found one. For start, all of the stories I wrote emerge from the same repeated love scenario, the boy meets the girl, and the girl falls in love with the boy. The only difference is the location, it could be a café, a bus stop, a library, or even an airport. You see the trick here, is that the location tells us something about who they are, whether they like coffee, or enjoy reading books. The characters of this story meet on a seashore, and the location doesn't really tell us anything because they both hate the beach. How they look like can also hint to what kind of love would develop. All these unnecessary details are added just to make it seem like the story is original. It is all to excite you for wanting to know what will possibly happen next. Wondering if you have ever or will ever be in a similar situation. Will your books accidentally fall in front of prince charming, and would he help you collect them? What happens next in this story is the first "I love you," that would feel special in some sort of way. If this story would be turned into a movie, the girl will tell you about how things suddenly paused. While the boy would tell you about how everything went blurry except for her face. They would tell you how things are falling into place, and how they are distant for one another. How they actually met would be exaggerated just so that it would sound like the perfect love scene from a movie. Later, we would know that the boy feels the same way, that they both experience the so-called never experienced before.

They would start to idolize one another, telling us about how the other is perfect. They would forget that they once were a whole and would call one another the other half. Like every love scenario, it would get boring for you to just watch these two being in love. Therefore, it is about time for misunderstandings and conflicts to arise leading the ship they went on to sink. In the middle of the night when the ship starts to sink, the boy departs on a separate boat, with the hope of getting back to the shore to build a new ship, a much stronger one. That even the biggest iceberg cannot break it. However, the story doesn't end up in that way. There have been many other boats in the open water. The girl wakes up the next day with confusion. She remains in the ship, trying to rebuild it, and not letting the passing boats help her fix it. The boy doesn't go back to the shore, he spent his time joining other boats and ships, having dinner, and spend some time with different people. Just hours later in the middle of the night, again he would flee in his boat looking for another exciting moment. The girl awaits him, and he continues trying to fool his heart believing that sparks are decided and not fated. So here my friends, the perfect departing line is an unresolved one or a so-called open ending.

People Always Leave

LETTER 11
Dear Al,

My only best friend, Munira, moved to the UK last year with her brother because her family has disappeared for getting involved with some something that I cannot write. I am not sure what the situation is but what I know is that no one was looking at them in the same way anymore. No one wants to be involved. I remember my parents telling me not to talk to her anymore... But I still messaged her. She never did anything bad to me.

Senior year. The time when you were a stranger to me again. Strangers become friends and friends become strangers. Munira visited again this year; she came to visit me. I knew she was coming, but my mother cannot know about this. I heard you were making fun of her because she is in trouble. I really do not know why everyone hates her. She didn't do anything; before her parents got into trouble everyone was treating them like royals because of how much money they had. Now she is treated like a cockroach... everyone is waiting to step on her. There is nowhere she belongs.

I am glad I got to see her. This time she had all my pieces of writing organised in a folder. She looked at me with a big smile. She said that I should be proud of myself for being able to write this much. I used to send her the same letters I am writing you write now but I am still afraid to send them.

You know... what Munira said? She told me she was proud of me for being able to write everything down... I have posted them on Wattpad but then I realised so many people from school were reading my thoughts. It didn't feel right. Munira told me that, as you turn the pages, I will see that not only did my writing improved but I changed.

My old way of writing did actually change as time passed. At that time, I used to listen to music to cope with losing: listening to The Script and focusing on words that I could relate to. I also use to watch the series 'One Tree Hill', and always felt like Peyton; she always writes things like 'People always leave'. We cannot stop a person from leaving simply because it is hard feeling left out and alone in confusion. I told her that I knew what had happened to her family. When I told her she looked at me and she suddenly went offline and her display picture was removed. Why would she walk away from me just because I knew the truth?

After that day, we both went our separate ways. She went to the UK to continue her studies. She also changed her passport and name. She says she wants to start a new life there with her brother. I do not understand what happened or what they did but I know that my best friend is gone. I respected that and I just watched her leave. I didn't know what I had done wrong though.

Yes, Al. People always leave.

Sometimes there are things I wish I hadn't said, maybe if I hadn't brought up her parents this wouldn't have happened. Things I wish I hadn't done. I feel like I don't know why she is part of this letter. She is or was a dear friend but not anymore. She is not here but I always feel like her shadow is still here telling me that I can do it. It is when I finally find a friend that the friend leaves. As soon as I get comfortable around some people, it all comes to an end.

I constantly try to remind myself that things will be okay. I know that she is meeting new people in the UK, and right now that I have stopped writing to her, I feel like that we are the furthest apart we have ever been since we became friends. But knowing that she is happy with her life is enough.

I left this letter midway through and now I am back to continue writing. I am writing this to try to understand why everyone would hurt me the way you did. What did I do wrong, that makes me not deserve at least this so-called 'closure', that I am looking for? I was very confused. I was writing to you more than I should've, and on every paper my thoughts were different, my interpretations of why we are strangers were different. I try to look at losing from every direction. Maybe, just maybe I thought, if you read my thoughts, you would think of me as a good person who you would rather keep in your life. And maybe if you do not want me to be part of your life at least you would explain why I got kicked out. I thought something was wrong with me. Maybe I wasn't a good person, or I constantly reminded you of the past. Maybe I was toxic to you. My head was full of 'maybes' and confusion. Maybe you were as lost as me, and now I understand that all my thoughts were just illusions after my stepfather's death. I knew you before my stepfather passed away and I know I cannot bring my stepfather back. But I thought maybe the only person that I could bring back from the past is you. But you never came back. You do not reply to me anymore. You became a stranger when I needed to talk because I needed a friend. Munira vanished too. Why? I know you are both not 'a friend' to me but all I know that I still needed you around. We all have weaknesses, but I knew I needed time, because, as a teenager it is bound to be hard to understand why people leave. Why people become just part of the past. People that shaped us and take care of us suddenly vanish into thin air. Even when my life changed and improved for the better. I felt like wanting to share my time with both of you. I no longer think you wanted to hear anything about what I want to say but there is just too much that I would want to share.

Every time I try to write to Al, I listen to my own echo again and again as it changes every time. It is too late to change anything. You already have an image of me, and I have a different image of you. You like to have a wall between us. I always wished we could just sit and talk again. I wanted to hear your side of the story. But it is pointless now, the time has passed, and it is now a long time ago. I think you don't remember me anymore. I cannot fix the past, but all I want sometimes is to hear the other side of the story. I wanted a reason for why you said you would always be here for me, no matter what, but then vanished. Why did your words and actions never align? I always went back mentally to you, sometimes wanting you to come back. Sometimes I just wanted to punch you in the face for ignoring me. I was confused about how I should feel and most importantly for why feelings are not even. You claim to know me better than anyone, but you never sat and had an actual conversation with me. You are always with people who despise me the most.

I forgive you for not knowing me. AL was like a wall that I talked to and all I hear are echoes of my thoughts. We were kids back then immaturely listening to people who just wanted to ruin our lives, people who didn't care about us. You still sit with them.

There are things that we need to overcome in life in order to reach our goals. One is facing the things that we are afraid of, to become stronger people. Rather than wasting time ignoring my own fear, I did what makes me feel better about myself. I put a face on my fear by identifying it; the fear of losing. I am who I am and I am becoming a much stronger person by accepting myself and enjoying my story. I am everything that I can be and maybe not everything that I want to be, but I am everything that I will need to be in this life. Overcoming my fear of loss means not wasting my time and opportunities to give back to the world. There is no limit to strength because right now we are not everything we want to be and that is okay. We waste so much time every day that we can use to develop ourselves. I decided to not spend the rest of my life grieving the past but rather enjoy the present while accepting that grief is part of living. I will experience grief from time to time, but this means that we have people in our life that are worth missing. I do not want to lose more time with the people who chose to stay every day.

Loss is not an enemy because it is a necessary part of life. We can never lose the fact that we once had something that meant so much to us. We all lose things every day, and as time passes we will master the art of losing, which is discussed in Elizabeth Bishop's poem One Art:

'The art of losing isn't hard to master; so many things seem filled with the intent to be lost that their loss is no

disaster. Lose something every day. Accept the fluster of lost door keys, the hour badly spent. The art of losing isn't hard to master.'

As we grow older, we will lose many things, and, as Bishop says, when we lose many things, we master the art of losing. Then we will not be afraid of losing anymore. I remember losing my Barbie doll and how upset I was. We lose many things. We lose time as it passes by. We lose years as we age. More important than anything else, we lose ourselves. We cannot feel sad when we lose something. Instead, we should focus on what we have, and the need to love ourselves.

I have so many good people in my life, I have to stop looking at what I don't have and focus on what I have. Maybe you can master loss by losing something every day but you are also gaining something every day. You gain new experiences, meet new people, and learn new things. Enjoy life to the fullest, make time for your friends and family, and learn something new every day.

The best part of writing all of this down is the feeling I have afterward. I feel like I just got out of a hole of sadness... but the writing wasn't what pulled me out. It was reading different philosophies of death. When you are sad, you shouldn't become superficial; you should dig further to understand more. God gave us a brain to learn more and to realise we should dedicate our wealth to helping others because some people have it worse. I remember an immigrant who slept on a train; he fell off the train and died. It made me realise how selfish we can be when we are thinking about our sorrow. Instead we can give, and when we give our sorrow will not matter so much. We should learn to let go of things and do good because, when you give, you reach the state of mind where you feel like nothing really matters.

My grandfather is still alive, but he doesn't walk anymore so he is usually in his wheelchair. He is usually quiet but, even if he doesn't recall who we are, he still sings the same Emirati songs and asks for almost three cups of coffee a day. Some days he complains that the coffee is cold. He likes his coffee a certain way. He remembers the things he loves. He is still the same person he once was inside. He didn't lose his identity; instead, he remained the same. My mother just got a marriage proposal from a businessman in the US and I am insisting that she goes and lives her life. Things that happen to us can change the road of life we are walking on. It is just like a turn in the road that can change our interest and our passion.

I found Munira's Instagram account by searching using her email. I found out that she has changed her name to Monica. And she has changed her black hair to light brown hair with green highlights. In one of the pictures, she was wearing a red sweater surrounded by new people. She was happy studying and working with people she cared about. I sometimes feel replaced, but at least I felt happy seeing her grow happily with people who didn't judge her. People who cared about her. Seeing her happy meant so much to me. I didn't want her to come back. I wanted her to stay happy. She was way happier than when she was here.

Al, our roads may not collide again, but I can be happy that they collided in the past. I care about you enough to see you happy, and I know that I was also happy in my life. I was surrounded by people who loved me and cared about me and Al was too. I am who I am and I am happy with that. There is no such thing as an end, because life is full of infinite endings.

I am letting it out so I can understand that I am a strong person and there are infinite tomorrows waiting for me. I will accept the endless possibilities.

We are all strong in our own way. We can handle anything if we believe that we can handle it. We should not fear being ourselves. This is the beginning of something new, new adventures either in this life or in the afterlife. I am letting go of these memories because there are infinite endings, and every time it seems like an ending, it is a new beginning. Losing people is not the end because we don't lose them. They live in us even if we don't really notice it. But they shape us. Rather than looking at losing people as something that makes me depressed, maybe I should look back with a smile feeling happy for once having had them in my life.

Graduation day will probably be the last time I see you, Al. It will be the last time I write you a letter, but we are graduating in a month.

It will be our last goodbye.

I forgive you... for not taking the chance to be patient with me. I know that even if you do not show it, or even act like it, you are a good person. You are chased by your own demons.

You are the reason I started to write, but not the reason that I keep writing. I am grateful for that. One day, I will move to New York City, and I will make art.

We all make mistakes.

Some mistakes turn into memories.

You are now just a memory.

A nice memory that I do not regret... Goodbye, Al.

I Wish

AL
I wish this was not the last goodbye.

MEDYA
But it was our last goodbye.

AL
I cannot let this happen. It wasn't our last goodbye, and I am glad that I tried to make things right. I am glad that I fought fate and walked back. I am glad I spent the next several years with you. Our last goodbye was the day when you were gone.

MEDYA
You let go of me way before that. You moved on. You were jumping from one relationship to the next. You never came back.

AL
No, it wasn't. It shouldn't have ended this way. I still remember the taste of the pancakes. That tragic morning, you made me my favourite blueberry pancakes for breakfast. I remember everything in detail; there were three pieces of

pancakes filled with blueberries all covered with a drizzle of honey... the one your friend brought from Saudi.

MEDYA
If you still want me, why did you let me go?

AL
This is what happened. You asked me to book your favourite restaurant because you wanted to tell me something. I remember I booked it at 7:00 pm. I went to work; I was in a good mood because we had made a lot of money from the last deal we had done. Everything was great until I received a call from the hospital. I went straight to the car and called Ash. I remember her stuttering, saying that you are gone. Ash came right away that day. You just need to believe that this is how it ended. I ran into the hospital but I was late. They asked me if I wanted to see you, but I couldn't. I was afraid. I was afraid of losing everything that matters to me. I wasn't moving at all. I loved you. I always did.

I couldn't stay, I just went back home. I wanted to be alone. Everything was hard to process. Why is it when everything is okay everything is suddenly taken away? I need to stop talking to the ghost of you. Stop hunting my head.

The funeral was at our house. Munira didn't come. I wanted to talk to her, I wanted her to tell me what the last things were you had talked about, because there was a call on our living room phone that was from the UK for a couple of minutes the day before she passed away.

I told Aisha to get me in contact with Munira, but she told me she was never close to Medya. I went to the room, and I looked through her laptop trying to find a way to contact

Munira. I tried calling the UK number but no one picked up. So, I emailed her saying that we really needed to talk.

A month later…

I heard a knock on the door. It was Munira.

"Yes, Al. We need to talk."

I grabbed two mugs and poured some coffee.

She looked at me and said, "Are you doing, okay?"

"I cannot get her out of my head." I paused for a few seconds then looked back at Munira, and asked: "Why do we lose people we love?"

"Al… you do not lose people, you just learn to let them go," she said.

"She chose him. Why did she choose him?" I yelled.

"I wouldn't want her to be with you," she said.

"What did I do for you to hate me?" I asked.

"The letters that are in the blue box I am carrying with me. You received these letters," she said.

"What letters?" I asked confused.

"Didn't you read them?" She looked at me, clearly confused.

"I didn't," I responded while I was trying to think about which letters she was talking about.

"They were addressed to you. Didn't she send them? I am sure she did!" she said.

"I don't want to hear about these letters, and I don't know what you are talking about," I said coldly.

She put the box on the table and left.

Goodbye

MEDYA

Letters are a collection of what we knew, what we know now, and what we wish we knew better. They help us connect with our old self, and, possibly, fulfil the emptiness conquering us inside. How can you ever make sense out of losing yourself before figuring out who you are? Who are we other than a collection of actions and words combined with each other, creating this image called life?

Nothing lasts forever, only a few things last for a while; they will all be gone in one way or another. That is why we need to appreciate what we have while we still have it. What makes moments valuable is the fact that they will eventually come to an end. Although this might seem like an optimistic approach at first glance, the realization that nothing is permanent and no moment is forever makes us more aware of 'now', rather than 'back then'. I do not know what I am going to do next, as nothing ever goes according to plan. Gratitude takes a lot of pain. Losing the battle to the unknown takes time for you to let go of what could have been.

Al, you are the true ghost in the story, a shadow, that lacks any depth or emotion. You ghosted me and made me feel worthless, and ghosting has everything to do with the dead.

AL

I have decided to go back home because the time has come. I went to work, resigned from my job, then I packed my bags. I chose the first flight available. She chose him. I lost the battle of love, but that is the sort of feeling that creates the kind of art you want to see. Art awakens my soul, as it causes a vibration that makes me feel alive with emotion. I will try to project the rhythm of my grief into a series of paintings. I know that this is something that she would love and probably appreciate if she was around. It is time to focus on now. Thank you, New York City.

Our time together was just ours. It is our own creation. It must be like I'm in your dream, and you are in mine, or something. The stories are different, and the feelings are otherworldly.

DIRECTOR

End Scene. Great. We might have to practice this but let's organise it a little bit more. There is one thing that doesn't add up. Both of you carry so many feelings for each other but there has been all this miscommunication? Why didn't you give each other a chance to talk sometime in the past ten years?

MEDYA
His ego.

AL
Her pride.